Y0-EIY-899

To Bev D.!

Best wishes

+ Best of health!

Kevin Ferguson, MD

The Living Ancestor™

Seventeen Lessons for Defeating Health Problems and Living a Longer, Healthier Life.

Kevin W. Fergusson, MD

A DrPEN® Patient Education Book Selection

DrPEN Publishing, LLC

FIRST DrPEN PUBLISHING, LLC EDITION, MAY 2002

This publication is designed to provide information in regard to the Subject Matter covered. It is sold with the understanding that the publisher is not engaged in rendering medical, legal, or other professional service. If medical advice, legal advice, or other expert assistance is required, the service of a competent professional person should be sought.

Copyright ©2002 by Kevin W. Fergusson, MD

All rights reserved under International and Pan-American Copyright Conventions. No part of this publication may be reproduced, stored in a retrieval system, or transmitted, in any form or by any means, electronic, mechanical, photocopying, recording, or otherwise, without the prior written permission of the publisher.
Published in the United States by DrPEN Publishing, LLC,
Kogerama Building, 1501 Santa Rosa Road, Suite C-4, Richmond, VA 23229.

The Living Ancestor™, The Doctors' Patient Education Network, DrPEN®, DrPEN.com, DrPEN Publishing, LLC, and The Labcoat Librarian™ are trademarks of DrPEN, Inc.

Fergusson, Kevin W.
The Living Ancestor : seventeen lessons for defeating health problems
and living a longer, healthier life / Kevin W. Fergusson.
–1st ed. p. cm.

LCCN 202105979
ISBN 0-9720814-0-2

1. Longevity–Fiction. 2. Medicine–Fiction.
3. Health–Fiction. I. Title.

PS3606.E748L58 2002
813'.6 QBI33-563

Printed in the United States of America

Visit us on the World Wide Web at

www.drpen.com

Dedicated To

Theodore, Vivien, and Jane. May each be blessed with a long and healthy life full of wisdom and happiness.

TABLE *of* CONTENTS

Prologue 1

Chapter 1 The Discovery 3

Chapter 2 Tom's Best Friend 9

Chapter 3 Choose Your Battles 19

Chapter 4 The Doctor 27

Chapter 5 Life's Most Valuable Lessons 37

Chapter 6 The Attack 45

Chapter 7 The Foundation 53

Chapter 8 Friend or Foe 63

Chapter 9 The Living Ancestor 69

Chapter 10 The Window of Opportunity 83

Chapter 11 Surgery 91

Chapter 12 Adaptation 99

Chapter 13 The Power of the Name 107

Chapter 14 The Report 115

Chapter 15 Strategy and Tactics 121

Chapter 16 The Advocate 131

Chapter 17 The Gift 139

Epilogue 145

Postscript 147

Appendix A 149

Appendix B 151

Acknowledgments 155

Have you ever visited your doctor looking for help, but left feeling like the physician just didn't understand your particular problem? Do you know what to expect from physicians? Just as important, do you know what your physicians expect from you? Have you ever left your doctor's office understanding what he or she wanted you to do, but didn't understand why . . . so you didn't follow through all the way, then felt guilty? Have you ever visited your doctor afraid of what may be wrong with you, but felt a little intimidated and insecure so that you just couldn't tell the doctor your fears?

You are not alone. The manner in which health care is delivered today has changed. One of the reasons for that change is the explosive growth of medical knowledge that requires physicians to use networks of specialists to deliver all the care you may require. Although this system is more powerful, it is not always "patient friendly," and sometimes real needs slip through the cracks.

With all the specialized knowledge and skills available to you today, your basic need remains the same: You need someone to understand what's wrong and to help. But unlike the patients and caregivers of previous generations, you are no longer content to be a passive recipient of healthcare services. You are seeking information and asking questions. You are wise to do so, but sometimes you become frustrated when you are confused by the flood of health information now available through the media.

You want to be fully informed without being needlessly frightened.

You want to participate in the medical decisions that affect your life and the lives of your family. And even though the healthcare process is more complex, you want to understand as best you can and be treated with respect. After all, it's either you or the one you are caring for that needs help, not the doctor.

What you lack is a strategic way of approaching the healthcare system with all its complexities of primary and specialized care. That is why I have written this book. *The Living Ancestor*™ presents the strategy you need to work together with your physicians, hospitals, and other health professionals to achieve the best possible outcomes. Follow the Living Ancestor™ and discover the secrets of success in the battle against disease.

I hope you find *The Living Ancestor*™ an inspiration and a helpful guide to living a long and happy life.

KEVIN W. FERGUSSON, MD

Founder, DrPEN, Inc.
The Doctors' Patient Education Network™

CHAPTER I

The Discovery

"A man of knowledge understands others, a man of wisdom also understands himself."

—Lao-tzu (604 BC - 531 BC)

"Uh, Dr. Kong?"

Dr. Jian-Shou Kong turned to look at the young student in the third row. Although retired from the practice of medicine, he still taught first year medical students patient interviewing and communication skills.

"Yes, Miss Freeman."

"I understand what you're saying, but I wonder, umm..."

"Wonder what, Miss Freeman?"

"It's just that, well, I'm going to med school because I want to learn how the body works. You know, biology…the science of medicine more than the art of talking with patients. I think that's why we're all here." She glanced around the room for a symbolic show of hands.

"Green wood is hard to burn; the inexperienced are difficult to teach," Dr. Kong replied, more an observation than an answer. At just 5 feet 6 inches tall and lean as a rail, he was a man of advanced years, but like so many Asians, quick of mind and ageless.

"Seriously, Dr. Kong. I feel like I'm wasting my time here. Anatomy, physiology, pathology – that's what I'm here to learn. After all, I've been talking with people all my life!"

"I'm sure you have."

A mild ripple of laughter rose among the students in the small arena classroom. "Yes, yes, I know," said Dr. Kong, bringing the class back to the issue. "The knowledge and skill of the physician are made effective through a relationship with the patient. In fact, *all* services are delivered through a relationship with a patient and a health professional – a physician, a nurse, a therapist, and so on."

He paused for a few seconds to read their faces. Seeing little understanding, he continued a lecture he had given many times to other classes at the Georgetown University Medical School. This relationship, he explained, has a profound effect on the care given to the patient. Despite the highest skills of the health professional, if the relationship does not satisfy the needs and expectations of the patient, then the care offered falls short.

A study by the Pfizer Medical Humanities Initiative showed that positive patient-physician relationships tend to form when physicians "provide fast and efficient medical treatment, establish friendly rapport, and show compassion," and when patients "are honest, take an active interest in their own health, and keep track of the medications they are taking."

This time it was Mr. Hillman who spoke up. "You mean I should expect my patients to *help* me take care of them?"

"Of course," Dr. Kong replied.

"But most patients don't want to do that. They just want to get fixed up so they can go back and do whatever they were doing ..."

"Yes," added Jennifer in the back row, "even if what they're doing is why they got sick in the first place."

"As your generation would say, 'Isn't that awesome!'" Dr. Kong said with a smile. Another round of laughter seemed to break the tension. "But you must understand, the roles of physicians and patients are changing. Most patients no longer want a fatherly authoritative physician to issue commands they blindly follow."

"As long as they don't expect house calls," chimed in Michael, the class entertainer.

"What *do* they want?" asked the always-serious Jenna in the front row.

"Patients sense that the body of knowledge of medicine has grown too large for any one physician to grasp completely and that health care today often means using teams of professionals working together for the best outcome, with the patient's needs determining the members of the team."

It was now open mike in the classroom.

"I hear residents and even attending physicians talk, and they seem pretty cynical," said Steve.

"How so?" asked Dr. Kong.

"Well, sometimes they complain about the insurance rules and the new clinical pathways mandated by the hospital. But, you know, they also complain about patients and how they still want them to be the kind, compassionate "savior" who'll get them well and back on their feet again."

"Ah, the Kindly Doctor Welby Syndrome," added Paul. "They watch too much Nick at Nite."

Grace Freeman again: "Seriously. The insurance companies constantly pressure doctors to lower their fees, see more patients, and question their utilization of services. I get the sense physicians are questioning whether it's still worth the effort to invest time in meaningful relationships with patients when the patient may be forced to find a new doctor, you know, just because his employer chooses a new insurance plan."

"Another thing," added Rich. "The media barrage patients with so much healthcare information, they don't know what to believe."

"Who teaches the patients? The media?" asked Dr. Kong.

"Well, the media sure give patients a lot of information, mostly incomplete, and now the Internet ..."

"Excuse me," interjected Dr. Kong, "Having a great deal of information differs from learning. But getting back to you as medical students, do you become a competent physician from going to class, memorizing information, and passing all the tests?"

"Well, that's what we do everyday," answered Paul a bit defensively.

"True. But you will not become a competent physician until you learn how to apply knowledge to accomplish appropriate goals." Dr. Kong explained that information doesn't help patients unless they learn how to apply it to improve their health. Physicians help patients establish the goals of learning that are relevant to patient problems. "So who teaches the patients? Are they left to teach themselves?"

"Dr. Kong, it sounds like you're saying patients need a book or something that approaches illness from the patient's perspective, rather than from the physician's," said Jenna, as if that might be the answer to her question.

Dr. Kong paused, and the students sensed he was no longer present but remembering some event long past. The words of Carl Jung from Dr. Kong's college days slowly surfaced. He closed his eyes. 'Enlightenment comes not from imaging figures of light, but from making the darkness conscious.' Dr. Kong reopened his eyes.

"My esteemed students, Confucius said, 'To know that you know, and to know that you don't know–that is real wisdom.'"

The students glanced at each other as clueless as before. Dr. Kong did not explain his thoughts to his students, but that day he had made a discovery. He had devoted his academic career as a physician to teaching medical students the art of communication with patients. Now the question began to form in his mind–a question he knew he would someday answer for everyone who cared to learn the answer:

Can patients be taught how to approach illness from their own perspective, rather than from the perspective of the professional?

LESSON ONE

Healing happens through relationships, primarily the patient-physician relationship, the patient-nurse relationship, and other patient-health professional relationships.* Create and nurture these relationships.

**Although health professionals assist you in making the crucial healthcare decisions, understand and appreciate that your caregivers are your friends and family. They will take care of 80% of your healthcare needs.*

CHAPTER 2

Tom's Best Friend

"To handle difficulties, handle them when they are small and just beginning."

—LAO-TZU (604 BC - 531 BC)

"Bill, do you feel OK?" asked his wife, Susan. Bill Wallace was sitting quietly in the family room when Susan got home from work. Normally, he would be reading the newspaper or watching TV. She had been worried about him for several weeks now because of his chronic attacks of indigestion and had been trying to get him to go see a doctor. Bill, on the other hand, kept pumping antacids and insisting there was nothing wrong with him. *Men are so pig-headed,* Susan thought.

"I'm all right, I think. Tom and I were playing racquetball this afternoon, but that indigestion finally got so bad I just had to quit. I guess I'm not 20 anymore." Tom Chance was Bill's best friend. They had hung out together since high school and now had kids about the same age.

"You look kind of pale. I'll get you a glass of water." Susan put down her briefcase and stepped into the kitchen.

Suddenly, Bill felt a crushing pain across his chest. It felt like an invisible hand had reached inside his chest, grabbed the walls of his heart, and kept squeezing tighter and tighter. The room closed in on him and he could barely get the cry out, "Susan!" before the room faded into darkness.

Susan heard the fall from the kitchen and rushed to the figure clumped on the floor. "Oh my God!" Bill! Bill!" There was no answer. His skin was soaking wet and a sickly white. She pushed him onto his back and frantically tried to find a pulse. "Don't you die on me!" She thumped him on the chest like she had seen the doctors do on "ER." Nothing. She tried to loosen his shirt.

"Mom, what's going on!" She had not heard their 13-year-old son come in from the backdoor. He saw his mom bent over his dad and froze.

"Daniel, call 911. Quick! I think Dad's having a heart attack!" Daniel ran for the phone.

Susan tried to do CPR but she really didn't know how to do it. Every time she tried to blow into Bill's mouth she felt the air just coming out his nose. She tried pinching it, but could tell something was blocking the air from getting to the lungs. Bill weighed over 200 pounds, and she felt so incompetent and inadequate as she tried to push on his chest like she'd seen on TV.

Daniel ran back into the room, panic stricken. "They're on their way. What can I do?"

"Go next door and see if Mrs. Carter is home, then wait out front for the rescue squad."

Daniel stood there in a state of shock looking at his Dad lying on the floor. Some foam was coming out of the side of his mouth, and his lips were turning an unnatural reddish-purple.

"Daniel, please!" Susan raised her voice and looked up at him through wet eyes.

Daniel shook his head.

"Go and find Mrs. Carter, OK!" she tried to inject some kindness and concern for Daniel into her voice. Daniel ran next door leaving the front door wide open.

Oh, Bill. Why didn't you listen to me and go see the doctor, Susan said to herself, angry, frustrated, and scared all at the same time.

It seemed like hours to Susan, but three paramedics from the nearby rescue squad arrived within 10 minutes. They carried cases containing medical equipment and vials of drugs. Susan backed away. She had been able to remain fairly calm because of the demand for action, but now the fear began to rise again and she had trouble controlling the tremor in her hands. They stripped his shirt and exposed the chest.

"We don't have time for leads, Kirk. Let's get the rhythm from the paddles," the older paramedic said.

Kirk squeezed some jelly on Bill's chest and put two paddles on the chest, one on the top, the other on the left. "He's in a coarse V-fib."

"Shock him at 200," Harry, the head paramedic, ordered as he got a long plastic tube and a curved metal instrument out of a bag. Jack, the other paramedic, was doing chest compressions.

"All clear!" Susan saw the chest jump off the floor as the paramedic released the electrical shock, then smelt the faint, sickening odor of burned flesh.

"Nothing," said Kirk.

"Shock him again at 300," said Harry as he moved over to Bill's head. Kirk recharged the paddles.

"All clear." Bill's chest jumped again and the odor was stronger. "Still nothing."

Harry inserted the curved instrument into Bill's throat. Susan could see the Adam's apple being lifted up and a light shining through the skin in his throat. Harry quickly inserted the plastic tube and taped it in place, then began to hyperventilate Bill's lungs.

"We don't have time for an IV. Not yet. Let's give him some epi down the tube." Harry took off the balloon attachment and shot a large IV of clear medicine down into Bill's lungs. "Let's shock him again at 360."

Again Susan saw the chest convulse at the electrical shock.

"We've got a rhythm, Harry," said Kirk. "Looks like sinus."

"Hold the compressions. Any pulse?" asked Harry.

"Yea, faint one."

Susan thought Bill's lips looked less purple.

"Jack, see if you can get an IV on him. We need to give him some lidocaine. Kirk, get the stretcher."

Harry began to question Susan. "Has he been having any problems lately that you know of, ma'am?"

"He's been complaining of a lot of heartburn lately. He played racquetball earlier today. Said he had to stop early because it got so bad. You know, the heartburn. Will he be OK?"

Harry was noncommittal. The pupils of Bill's eyes were dilated, but he had not had time to see if they responded to light. *Why don't these guys ever learn the warning signs of heart disease,* Harry thought to himself. *It's the number one killer in the U.S. and everyone denies it could happen to them.* He tried to give Susan an encouraging smile, but he knew the guy had been down a long time. "We'll get him to the hospital as soon as we can."

"Tom, Sue Wallace just called from the hospital. Bill's had a heart attack. He's in the Coronary Care Unit at St. Bernadine's."

Tom was dumbstruck. "You're kidding. We were just playing racquetball this afternoon. What happened?"

"Apparently, he hadn't been feeling well for the past few weeks, but he thought it was just indigestion."

"He didn't say anything to me about it."

"Well, that's no surprise! You guys are pretty stubborn, you know. I've been trying to get you to go see about that mole on your neck for a couple of months now." Linda was upset by the phone call, and she said it a little more spitefully than she intended.

Tom got up and raised his hand as if to say, *Get off my back*, but said nothing and went to get his jacket. "I'm going to go to the hospital."

"I am too," said Linda. Susan was one of her best friends.

When they arrived at the CCU, they were told that only immediate family members could go inside, so they sat in the waiting room until Susan and Daniel came back out. They noticed an attractive young woman in a short white lab coat sitting quietly in the corner. Tom glanced over and saw on her name tag, "Grace Freeman, Medicine-2005," and figured out she was a medical student. He was surprised she wasn't doing anything, just staring at the floor.

"Tom ... Linda ..." Susan looked devastated as she entered the room with her arm around Daniel.

"Sue ... how's Bill?" Linda rushed to her friend, but her answer made Linda's knees wobble.

"He's gone," Susan cried out, biting her lower lip and trying to maintain her composure.

"Oh Susan, I'm so sorry," said Linda as she hugged her.

Tom didn't know what to say. He was in shock. It was too sudden, too final.

The medical student in the corner tried to get up and leave, but Susan saw her out of the corner of her eye and called out to her,

"Grace, just a minute. Excuse me, Linda," Susan whispered. Linda put her arm around Daniel as Susan went over to talk to Grace. The attending physicians had not been able to spend much time with the family, but Grace Freeman had been with them almost every minute over the last two hours, explaining what was happening.

Susan clasped Grace's hands, but Grace had trouble looking up. It was her first death as a medical student, and she didn't know how to handle it. Doing an early clinical rotation, she had been assigned to the case and had followed it from the ER to the CCU. But she had not yet learned how to shield her emotions from her work, and her eyes welled with tears.

"I'm so sorry, Mrs. Wallace."

Susan gave Grace's hand a squeeze. It was too early for her to feel the true impact of the loss of her husband, and her natural instincts as a mother stirred within her, making her feel more in control than would be expected. "I know. Everyone did their best. That's all you can do. Just helping us understand what's going on ... you've helped us more than you know."

The young girl looked up, but didn't know what to say. Why was this poor woman comforting *her?* She felt embarrassed and ashamed– and unprofessional.

"You're going to be a good doctor, honey. You've got a good heart, OK?"

"Again, I'm so sorry. And thanks." This was an experience the future Grace Freeman, M.D. would remember for life.

Susan let her go and Linda came over and put her arm

around her.

"Sue, would you like some coffee or something? Let's all go down to the cafeteria, OK?"

"I have to get Bill's things and ..."

"I'll talk to the nurse. We'll come back later."

"Sure."

Conversation was awkward, but Linda knew that just being there was more important than saying anything. Tom sat quietly. He still didn't know what to say. It really hadn't sunk in that his best friend was really gone until he looked over at Daniel and saw the same feelings of anger and fear he had felt at the same age when he had lost his father in the same way 30 years ago. He knew the emotional wounds from this day would linger for years. No one can replace a father.

LESSON TWO

Know the early warning signs of disease. For information on heart disease see Appendix A at the back of this book. For information on the early warning signs of other diseases go to: **www.drpen.com/warningsigns**

CHAPTER 3

Choose Your Battles

"To fight and conquer in all your battles is not supreme excellence; supreme excellence consists in breaking down resistance without fighting."

—SUN-TZU (~300 BC)

"Good Morning. This is Dr. Smith's office. How can I help you?"

"Yes. This is Linda Chance. I need to make an appointment with Dr. Smith for my husband, Tom Chance." The receptionist rolled her eyes and looked over at the coworker next to her. Pointing at the telephone she spoke with her lips, *It's her!*

"Mrs. Chance, I explained to you that Falls Church Family

Practice has a policy not to accept new patients who have either not shown up for their appointment or cancelled their appointments without being seen."

"But you don't understand. I know there is no excuse for my husband, but I've been on the Internet and this mole on his neck looks exactly like the pictures of a melanoma."

"Yes. I'm sure that may be true, Mrs. Chance, but that is the office policy. There is nothing I can do about it."

"Don't you people care?" Linda asked, pacing around the office in her home where she worked as an interior designer. "Why can't you get it? If I'm right he could die from this."

"Maybe he needs to see a dermatologist."

"If I could get him in to see a dermatologist I sure wouldn't be wasting my time on the phone with you. We have an HMO for insurance and he has to see Dr. Smith first. I called client relations and he is listed on Dr. Smith's panel. They say that Dr. Smith HAS to see him, but YOU won't schedule an appointment for him. What is your name?"

"Susie"

"Alright, Susie. Now do you want to be listed on the law suit when my husband dies from a melanoma?"

"Please hold. There's someone on the other line." After several minutes she came back on the phone. "I'll have to put you through to our office manager." Before Linda could reply, she cut her off and put her through to the office manager's phone.

Susie turned to Gail sitting next to her. "It's days like this that make me want to go get a job at a library. I'm going to go smoke a cigarette. I'll be back in just a minute."

Linda slammed down the phone. She had already left two messages with the office manager and neither had been returned. She tried to refocus on the design in front of her, but she was too upset. The phone rang.

"Mrs. Chance. This is June at Windsor Assisted Living."

"Yes. Good morning."

"I'm sorry to disturb you this morning, but Mrs. Chance is not feeling well, today."

"What's the problem?"

"We're not sure. She's running a low grade fever and is a little more confused than normal."

"Have you given her any Tylenol?"

"Yes, a couple of hours ago."

"Well, what do you suggest?"

"I think we need to get her to see the doctor, today."

Linda closed her eyes. No physician's office would see her on this short of a notice and this would make her third emergency room visit in a week. *We really need to get her into a nursing home,* she thought to herself, *these assisted living facilities are just not capable of handling her.*

"OK. Whatever we need to do."

"Yes, ma'am. I'll make the arrangements."

Linda tried to meditate for a minute when she thought to herself, *Somehow I've got to get around these front office people. I know, I'll call Beth. She was the one who recommended Dr. Smith in the first place.* Beth was married to a cardiologist in the community and was very active with the volunteers at the local hospital. Linda had been working with the volunteers for the last three years.

"Beth. Good morning, this is the Linda Chance. How are you doing?"

"I'm doing fine, honey. How are you?" Beth and her husband had come from Atlanta and Beth remained a bastion of southern gentility despite living along the silicon strip outside of D.C. Their youngest son worked at AOL.

"I'm doing OK, but my husband has kind of made a fool of himself and didn't keep his appointment with Dr. Smith, so now they're refusing to reschedule him. I was wondering if you had any suggestions."

"Oh. I'm sorry. Let me call Cindy, Dr. Smith's nurse, and see what I can do, OK?"

"That would be great." Linda sighed.

"OK. Are you coming in this week with the volunteers?"

"Yes. I'm scheduled to work Wednesday morning."

"OK. Great. I'll see you then. Bye."

"Good-bye."

Linda felt better and was able to get some work done. Her interior design business had been tremendously successful. She specialized in designing home offices, and with the growth of the Internet everyone wanted a home office where they could work from home as well as at the office.

After lunch, Linda was going over some new proposals when the phone rang.

"Linda?"

"Yes."

"This is Cindy from Dr. Smith's office."

"Oh. How are you? I am so glad to hear from you."

"I understand that you're worried about a mole on your husband's neck?"

"Yes. I really think he needs to be seen."

"OK. I went ahead and told the front office to schedule him for this Thursday at 3 o'clock. Would that work?"

"We'll make it work."

"OK. We're going to have to work him in, so he may have to wait a little bit."

"That's fine. He'll be there."

"Good. Talk to you later."

"Good-bye."

Linda hung up the phone and dialed Tom. "Tom?"

"Hey, Linda. What's up?"

"I was able to get an appointment for you on Thursday afternoon at 3 o'clock with Dr. Smith."

"Linda. I'm really busy. I told you about this big sales contract we're working on for a complete enterprise system."

"Listen, Tom. You missed one appointment and then cancelled the other one without even telling me. Do you want the same thing that happened to Bill to happen to you? Get with it. You need to see the doctor. Don't be stupid."

"OK. OK. I'll keep it." Tom didn't want to get into this argument just now. He knew she was already angry with him.

"Good. See you tonight. Bye-bye."

"Bye." Tom hung up the phone and shook his head. *It's best to choose your battles,* he thought to himself, then he got back to work making calls. He had an enormous capacity to block out distractions and to selectively hear what he wanted to hear, but he got the message this time and knew for peace's sake he had better keep the appointment.

LESSON THREE

The battle against disease is war. Single soldiers don't win wars. Everyone needs allies in the war against disease and illness.

CHAPTER 4

The Doctor

"Tom, don't forget you have a doctor's appointment," Linda called out.

"Gotta go, honey," Tom half-answered, reaching for his briefcase on the kitchen counter.

"It's this afternoon at three. Please don't cancel it."

"I won't. I promise."

"This is the third appointment I've made for you to see about that mole on the back of your neck."

"OK, OK! I said I'd keep it," Tom called out with uncharacteristic irritation as he rushed to the car. If he didn't beat the traffic, he was going to be late for the meeting. "I'll see you around 6:00."

Tom Chance had a lot on his mind as he made the half-hour drive from his home in Falls Church, Virginia to his office at General Software Solutions, Inc. in Alexandria. *I really think that mole has been there all my life. Or it's just an aging spot. After all, I'm 43 years old now. With a wife, two kids, a mortgage, and a demanding job, I don't have time to sit in a doctor's waiting room all afternoon.*

And then there was his mom, living alone, not eating much. He and Linda had just gotten her relocated into Windsor Assisted Living, and now it looks like she needs to be moved to a nursing home. These constant trips to the hospital are driving Linda nuts and Tom felt guilty because he didn't have time to deal with it. *I guess a nursing home would sure help take some of the pressure off. Now, on top of everything else, my boss wants that sales contract I've been working on for the past two months closed in the next few days. She's getting a lot of pressure to look good for this quarter.*

Tom had trouble concentrating at the morning staff meeting, but after several cups of coffee he felt better. Sometimes he felt like he lived on caffeine and nervous energy, although he still worked out at the club once a week. He really looked forward to it, and he always felt better afterwards, but his busy schedule added to the pressure even during workout times. Money had been tight the last few months, and tuition for schools was due in a few weeks. *I've got to close that contract,* he thought to himself.

"Yo! Tom, where are you?" his boss called out in front of everyone. Maria could really tighten the screws when she wanted to. "At work we need to focus on *work.* How are we doing on the Davis account?"

"*We* are doing OK.," he answered assertively. "We think *we* can close before the end of the month."

Maria decided to ignore the sarcasm. "Good. It's a large contract,and you know we need it. So let's try to get at least a letter of intent today or tomorrow."

"Sure," Tom nodded. *How do some people manage it all,* he asked himself. *I've taken courses on time management, and all they seem to do is show me how to squeeze a few more items into an already overloaded schedule.* He scratched the back of his neck and felt the small, painless bump growing there. It did feel a little bigger, but it didn't hurt. *Why do I have to see a primary care physician first anyway? It seems like I could save time by just going straight to a skin doctor. I don't understand all this managed care stuff. Anyway, maybe I can write up this proposal on my laptop in his waiting room. Besides, I haven't seen a doctor in 10 years, but Linda says he's good. She says he really listens and doesn't make you feel like a child or an idiot. Still, seeing doctors is always a little scary.*

Tom felt sleepy after a late lunch and nearly jumped out of his chair when the alarm in his handheld computer went off at 2:30. Linda had set the alarm just in case he forgot his 3:00 pm appointment with Dr. Smith. *Sometimes I think everybody else controls my life except me,* he muttered under his breath. He grabbed his laptop and ran out the back of his office to drive over to Dr. Smith's office.

"Are you a new patient?" the receptionist asked from behind the glass-enclosed counter.

"My family has been here before, but this is actually my first visit," Tom replied.

"Then I'll need you to take these forms and fill them out for us. It should take about fifteen minutes or so. Oh, and I'll need to make a copy of your insurance card and driver's license."

"My driver's license?"

"We use it to verify information. Now, please take a seat there and fill out these forms. Thank you," she said with a firm, bureaucratic smile.

Tom looked over at the distinguished looking Asian gentleman reading a newspaper. Tom always had a hard time guessing the age of Asians. The gentleman looked up and, catching Tom's eye, nodded briefly, then went back to reading his paper. Tom sat down and began filling out his forms.

"Dr. Kong," the nurse called.

"Yes?" The Asian man looked up.

Dr. Kong walked across the room. As he went back with the nurse he said, "Thanks for getting back with me on the phone the other day, Cindy. I know you and Dr. Smith are very busy, and I appreciate your taking care of me. Good fortune smiles on a cheerful spirit."

Cindy smiled. "Are you feeling better?"

"Yes, thank you."

She enjoyed seeing Dr. Kong and taking care of him. He always treated everyone in the office with respect.

"That's great. You look good. Take a seat here and Dr. Smith will be with you in a few moments."

Dr. Kong had retired from practicing medicine several years earlier, but he was still invited at times to lecture at Georgetown, and he served as a consultant for difficult cases. The professors respected his expertise in discovering the elusive diagnosis, but toward the end of his career he had devoted himself to understanding communication and the dynamics of the patient-physician relationship. Dr. Kong kept abreast of the constantly changing world of medicine. He understood that medical knowledge had grown so large, no one person could understand it all; but he also grasped the timeless, unchanging relationship between a patient and his physician.

Cindy, Dr. Smith's nurse, found most physicians to be difficult patients, but not Dr. Kong. He surprised her with his gentle manner and thoughtful appreciation for what nurses do. He kept them honest, though, and would always ask questions if he didn't understand. Sometimes she would jot down his little sayings and share them with her family. *Good fortune smiles on a cheerful spirit,* she thought to herself. Jeremy could sure brighten his disposition a little, she thought, and he might find things working out better for him in middle school instead of feeling rejected all the time. As he got older she found it increasingly difficult to keep him thinking in a positive direction. She had put her foot down and said no to violent video games in their home.

After Tom finished filling out the registration forms he turned on his notebook computer to work on the proposal. He felt a little warm and noticed that his brow was moist, so he loosened his tie. He had been having waves of perspiration for months now, sometimes wakening him at night, soaking his pillow.

"Mr. Chance," the nurse called. Tom saved the spreadsheet he was working on and closed the computer. "Dr. Smith will be with you in a few moments." She noticed he looked tired. Glancing down at his chart, she thought he looked a little older than his true age. "I know you're here for Dr. Smith to check out a mole, but we'd like to get your height and weight and check your blood pressure, OK?"

"Sure," Tom replied as he put his laptop back in the case.

"We saw Linda the other day. How's she doing?"

"Great, as always. And I believe you saw my son, Michael."

"Yes. He told me he had recently joined the chess club at the Freepoint Library. I wonder if my son, Jeremy, would be interested."

"It's a great activity. I'm going to take Michael this Friday. I think they meet on the first and third Friday night each month. Maybe we'll see you and Jeremy there."

The nurse loosened Tom's shirtsleeve and rolled it up to take his blood pressure. "138 over 88," she said.

"Is that good?"

"It's within the normal range, but at the upper limits. Try to exercise a bit more and watch your salt intake. Dr. Smith will be with you in a moment."

"Thanks," he replied as the nurse closed the door behind her.

When Dr. Smith entered the room, he paused, reached out his hand, and greeted Tom, looking him in the eye. "It's good to meet you, Mr. Chance."

"Please, call me Tom, doctor."

"OK." Sitting down on a stool he asked, "How can I help you today?"

"Well, my wife, Linda, wanted you to check out a mole on the back of my neck."

"Has it been there long?"

"I'm not really sure."

"Uh-huh. Hard to see the back of your neck."

Tom smiled, not sure whether the good doctor was pulling his leg or not. "Linda noticed it a few months ago. Personally, I think it's just an aging spot."

"OK, we'll take a look at it. I noticed this is your first appointment with me. Have you seen any other physicians in the last few years?"

"To be honest, Doc, I haven't seen any physicians for at least 10 years, but I've been in good health and I really don't have any complaints."

"That's great, but you know, I think it might not be a bad idea to set up a complete history and physical exam sometime. Medicine has changed a lot in the past 10 years. These days we can prevent a disease if the symptoms are caught early enough."

"Sure. I'll check my schedule."

"OK. Well, let me take a look at this mole." Dr. Smith took a position behind Tom's back, then held a magnifying glass and bright light on the dark growth and wrote down some notes on a piece of paper. Tom thought he was taking too much time and began to get a little nervous. His chest felt tight.

"What do you think, Doc? Does it look OK?"

Dr. Smith sat back down and looked up. "Well, Tom, some things about this mole reassure me, and other things trouble me. It looks the same on both sides, which means it has a normal symmetry, but the border becomes a little irregular, and the black color concerns me. Fortunately, it measures only a quarter-inch in diameter. All in all, I think it would be better to just go ahead and remove it so we can send it off to a pathologist – just to be sure it's OK."

"What's that involve?" Tom asked. He had hoped the doctor would just tell him it looked OK and that he didn't have to do anything else.

"We would numb it up, then remove it by cutting around and under the mole. You might need to have one or two stitches."

"Can't you just burn it off?"

"Well, sometimes we do that if we are sure of the diagnosis, but in this case it's better to send it off for a biopsy."

"OK. You're the doctor." Tom sometimes used humor in place of courage.

"Now, either I can do this procedure here in the office, or I can refer you to a specialist, which may take a couple of weeks to arrange. Either way, if the biopsy comes back positive, we would need to send you to a plastic surgeon who would go back and do a larger procedure to be sure that the excision was complete."

Tom didn't really hear any of the last part of what Dr. Smith said. He really hadn't been prepared in his mind for all this. "OK, Doc. Let's roll. Can you take it off here...today?"

"No. I really don't have time to do it right now. I schedule these procedures on Fridays. You can set up an appointment at the front desk as you leave."

"Fine."

"Is there anything else I can help you with?"

"No."

"Then I'll see you Friday. It was good meeting you, Tom.

Take care."

After Dr. Smith left the room, Tom scheduled the appointment and called Linda on his cell phone. "Hi, Linda. Tom. I'm just leaving Dr. Smith's office. He wants to take this mole off on Friday, so I scheduled it for 10 am. Maria's going to hit the roof, but if the doctor recommends it, we really don't have much choice."

"She'll get over it. Ten o'clock should work out OK. See you around six. Love you. Bye."

Tom clicked off and felt a sense of relief. He knew he shouldn't have put this off so long, and he felt relieved he had finally seen the doctor. Somehow, knowing the doctor was on his side gave him a sense of comfort. He decided to take what little was left of the afternoon off to work out at the gym and write up the proposal tonight at home. Taking a deep breath he felt a sense of peace that he had not felt for months.

A peace destined to be all too brief.

LESSON FOUR

Do not hope on illness not coming, but depend on yourself being prepared. The primary goal of the patient-physician relationship is to create an effective healing alliance. If you do not currently have a primary-care doctor, make an appointment. Do it today.

To find a family physician in your area go to:
http://familydoctor.org/cgi-bin/finddoc.pl
To find a board-certified pediatrician in your area go to:
http://www.abp.org/VERIFICA/Veritest.htm
To find other physicians go to the American Medical Association's DoctorFinder at:
http://www.ama-assn.org/aps/amahg.htm

CHAPTER 5

Life's Most Valuable Lessons

"Adversity teaches life's most valuable lessons.
A kite rises because of an opposing wind."

—Chinese Proverb

"Michael, are you ready to go? It's almost 6:30 and they set up at 7:00."

"Yeah, Dad. Just a second."

Fourteen-year-old Michael Chance was looking forward to going to the chess club. Some of his friends at school were getting into chess so he had joined the school club which met on Tuesday afternoons, but he had never been to any real competitions. The

Freepoint Library's club played competitive chess that used timers. Like most eighth graders, he was more competitive than realistic. He had read up on some of the more common openings and closings but was nervous about actually playing a live opponent for the first time. He grabbed his new chess set and vinyl roll-up board and rushed down the stairs.

The sutures on the back of Tom's neck irritated him some and he couldn't help picking at them. Dr. Smith had taken off the mole that morning. He needed to go back in ten days to have the stitches removed. Dr. Smith told him he did not need to restrict his activities; just try to keep the incision dry as much as possible. He said it was all right to take quick showers.

"Tom, you need to stop picking at it. I'm going to put a Band-Aid on it just to keep your fingers away," Linda scolded him.

I'm sure glad I got that letter of intent from Mr. Davis, Tom thought to himself. *Hopefully, we can close the deal the middle of next week just before the end of the month.* He felt things were looking up.

It had been years since Tom had played chess. When he was growing up he had enjoyed chess and was glad Michael was showing an interest in the game. He didn't mind at all the time he'd spend taking Michael to club matches. It might make for good father-son bonding. Anyway Michael needed more attention. Now that Sarah was living away from home at Brown University, Michael seemed to miss her big sister influence. Sarah was a real academic achiever, and Michael had always tried to keep up with her.

A meeting room at the Freeport Library had been set aside for the competition. Rows of tables had signs designating levels of play from novice to advanced. Boys and girls ranging in age from about 12 to 16 stood around the tables waiting for instructions. Parents hovered in the background as if unsure whether they should stay or leave the kids to their own fun. Michael drifted away from Tom and staked out a position at one of the beginner's tables where he immediately started talking to a cute blond girl about his age. Tom smiled. *Good opening move, Michael,* he thought, *and the games haven't even begun.* Looking around the audience of parents, Tom noticed an Asian gentleman across the room who was obviously older than the other adults. He looked familiar, and then it hit Tom. It was the same gentleman he had seen in Dr. Smith's waiting room that first visit.

"May I have your attention, please?" A man dressed in a cardigan sweater and tie raised his arms to get everyone's attention. When the talking died down, he continued. "I'm Frank Aldrich, president of the Freepoint Library Chess Club. I would like to welcome all of our new members and interested visitors joining us tonight. If you haven't done so, please write your name on one of the small pieces of paper at the front door and put it in the basket assigned for each level of skill. We will randomly assign players to begin the evening's competition according to their skill level." Michael and a handful of other newcomers made a beeline to the door to add their names to the hoppers.

"I would like to take a few moments to remind our new members of some basic rules. If you touch one of your own pieces, then you must play that piece. If you touch one of your opponent's pieces, you must capture that piece if you are able to do so. Tonight is coaches' night, and the players are allowed consultation with their coaches. Players will have 30 minutes each per game and will play a total of three games. Play runs fairly quick, so keep an eye on your time."

The baskets containing the players' names were brought to the front, and the pairings began. Michael was matched with a young boy his own age named Mark. Sitting next to Michael was an Asian-looking boy. Tom found a chair near the beginners' table and sat down to watch. The Asian gentleman sat next to him.

Tom nodded and asked, "Is that your son?"

The man smiled appreciatively and said, "Thank you, we care for him, but he is no pearl from an old oyster; he is my grandson."

"Of course," said Tom. Then, conscious of the need to maintain relative quiet during the matches, he whispered, "Have you been members of the club for long?"

"No, this is our second visit. An-Huan enjoys the game. I prefer Chinese Chess, which is played differently, but An-Huan was born here."

An-Huan came over to where the two were sitting, "Grandfather, I need some advice."

"Remember Sun Tzu. 'The superior strategist draws attention to the East, but launches his attack from the West.'"

"Yes, grandfather."

"Is your offspring playing?" asked Dr. Kong.

"Yes, my son. His name is Michael. He's sitting next to your grandson. I'm Tom Chance. I think I saw you the other day in Dr. Smith's office." Tom reached out his hand. Dr. Kong bowed his head slightly, and then as if catching himself, took Tom's hand and shook it. "Yes. Dr. Smith has been my personal physician for many years. Has your health been good?"

"Yes, no problem. I just had to have a small mole taken off. Dr. Smith did it this morning."

"Grandfather, I have captured two pawns and have a one knight advantage. His other knight has retreated and his pawns block me. I do not seem to be able to gain the center."

"'Do not attack great formations and avoid orderly ranks. Wait for opportunity. Search for weakness.'"

The boy stood curiously for a moment with his mind switching back and forth between two cultures and ways of thinking, then spoke with a knowing smile.

"Yes, grandfather, words like a guiding light over a darkened sea."

Tom listened to the advice with curiosity. His mind had trouble following Dr. Kong's thoughts so he looked over at the boy's board. The other player had arranged his pawns into a penetrating V-shape onto An-Huan's side of the board. The boy had a material advantage, but his position appeared weak.

Jian-Shou Kong leaned over and whispered in his grandson's ear, "War burns like fire. If you do not put it out, it will burn itself out."

In a surprise move An-Huan placed his white bishop into apparent jeopardy before the king's pawn. Tom could not understand the need for the sacrifice until he noticed the pawn was pinned by the white queen. The bishop had skirted along the outside of the pawn formation and was threatening attack on the black king smothered in the kingside corner. The boy would win on the next move. The swiftness of the attack had caught his opponent off guard, and he did not have time to defend his king.

Dr. Kong sat back in his chair to resume the conversation with Tom. "I am glad to hear you had Dr. Smith remove this mole. He is a wise tactician and never lays down strategy until he knows the nature of the enemy. You do well to trust him. Adversity teaches life's most valuable lessons. A kite rises because of an opposing wind."

The boys played two other games before Mr. Aldrich called out, "May I have your attention, please? We've had an enjoyable evening, but it is time to finish now. We will meet again on the third Friday of this month. I look forward to seeing you again then. Remember, at the next meeting the coaches will not be allowed to give advice during the competition. Good-bye."

Tom rose and spotted Michael talking again to the winsome blond girl. Checkmate! "Dr. Kong, I've enjoyed meeting you, and I hope to see you again soon."

"Yes, Mr. Chance. I also enjoyed meeting you. May your years grow as high as the mountains, and your heart be as peaceful as still waters." Bowing slightly he took An-Huan's hand and left.

May your years grow as high as the mountains, and your heart be as peaceful as still waters, Tom thought to himself and smiled. Interesting. They certainly say good-bye in an unusual way in China.

"Hey, Michael. How did you do? I was busy talking and got a little distracted. Did you win?"

"Yeah, Dad. Actually, I did. Mr. Long from school coached me a little bit and I did OK."

"That's great. Let's head home."

Lying in bed that night, Tom had a little trouble turning his mind off and going to sleep. The small wound stung where it rested against the pillow. He thought about his friend Bill and how little warning he had of a heart attack. Would he have acted differently to the chronic indigestion that signaled the problem? Probably not, he had to admit, but Linda wouldn't have given him a moment's peace about it. His mind kept drifting back to his conversation with Dr. Kong. *Adversity teaches life's most valuable lessons. A kite rises because of an opposing wind.* Tom did not naturally think in terms of enemies and alliances. He felt uncomfortable. He had always followed a relatively straight path in life. Do well in school. Get a good job. Work hard. Be independent. *Well, one thing's for sure. Dr. Kong's grandson certainly plays a strategic game of chess, but I'll never be able to remember his name, An-on something.* Tom finally drifted off to sleep, but he did not rest comfortably and kept having dreams of chess with his king continually being threatened while his men were pinned and unable to move.

LESSON FIVE

Illness is an adversity, and adversity teaches us life's most valuable lessons. Life is precious. Defend it! Fight for it!

CHAPTER 6

The Attack

"The person with courage and boldness, dares to die,
The person with courage and reserve, dares to live."

—LAO-TZU (604 BC - 531 BC)

"Mr. Chance, your wife is on line 3," the secretary, Judy, called on his intercom.

"Okay, Judy, thanks," Tom answered. Then he punched line 3.

"Hi Honey, what's up. Is everything OK?'

"Hi, Tom, I'm fine. Dr. Smith's office just called and said he had the report back on that mole. He would like to see both of us in his office together around 5 o'clock.

"Today?" Tom glanced at his day calendar.

"Uh-huh."

Tom didn't know whether to feel annoyed or frightened. "Well, did they say what was wrong? I'm supposed to see him in three days anyway to have the stitches taken out. Couldn't I just see him then?"

"They wouldn't tell me over the phone, but my guess is the report did not come back as well as we expected."

"Yeah, well, OK. I'll meet you at his office at five." Tom could tell from the tone of her voice she was nervous. The last time he had heard that tone was when Michael had been sick in the hospital with viral meningitis. He was only two years old then. Tom could still remember the feelings of helplessness, as Michael kept getting sicker and sicker. Just thinking back on it made Tom feel a tightness in his chest that went up into the back of his throat. Hospitals made him anxious; so did doctors' offices. He noticed his palms were wet, and he was having another one of those waves of perspiration he had been having for the past several months.

"Judy, I need to cancel my meeting with Douglas Wayne at 3:30. Something's come up. Could you please call his office and see if we can reschedule for early next week?"

"I'll try. Is everything OK?"

"Yeah. We're fine. Nothing major. Thanks." He clicked on his computer and distracted himself with status reports until 4:30 pm.

An eerily empty waiting room greeted Linda and Tom when they arrived. It gave both of them a sense of discomfort, a sense of being in the right place at the wrong time.

"Mr. and Mrs. Chance, if you would come back with me to Dr. Smith's office, he will be with you in just a moment. He's with his last patient for the day now." Cindy smiled at them, but didn't offer any other conversation. Tom got the sense she was under orders not to talk about medical things until after they had seen the doctor.

"You can both sit here. Dr. Smith should be with you in a few minutes."

"Thanks, Cindy," Linda replied.

"You're welcome."

Dr. Smith entered the room and sat down. Tom felt another wave of perspiration and noticed his heart was pounding. *I need to work out more*, he said to himself, with a sense of guilt.

Looking up at them, Dr. Smith began, "Thanks for changing your schedules around to meet with me. I know you're both very busy. I got the report back from the laboratory late yesterday afternoon. Unfortunately, Mr. Chance, it came back positive. This means that we are going to need to refer you to a plastic surgeon to remove a wider area. We don't do that type of procedure here in our office." Tom got the feeling Dr. Smith was trying to determine their reaction to what he was saying and was choosing his words very carefully.

"Dr. Smith," Linda interrupted, "I don't think Tom understands. What exactly does 'positive' mean?"

"Well, Linda, that's why I wanted to talk to both of you so that you would understand. Tom's biopsy came back showing this mole was a melanoma."

"What does 'melanoma' mean?" Tom asked, following Linda's lead.

"A melanoma is a type of skin cancer. It can occur anywhere to anyone, but Tom, you have a fairly high risk for skin cancer. Fortunately, this mole had not gotten very big before I removed it. Since I did a fairly wide excisional biopsy, it has probably been completely removed already, but studies have shown that the prognosis is best if a surgeon removes the whole area for about an inch or so in diameter around the previous biopsy and a pathologist looks at it through a microscope. This helps us be sure the melanoma has not spread beyond the borders of where I did the biopsy."

"I see," said Linda. Tom only heard the words 'skin cancer.' He had not heard the rest of the explanation.

"In this case, if the repeat excision by the plastic surgeon shows no further evidence of the melanoma, the prognosis is actually very good. The five-year survival rate is 98-100%. I will write this down for you in case you want to learn more about malignant melanomas." Taking out his prescription pad, Dr. Smith wrote down:

Malignant Melanoma
Clark's Level II
Breslow Thickness 0.55 mm
Stage I

Standing up from his desk he handed the paper to Tom. "Tom, I'm going to need to see you on a more regular basis to keep a closer eye on things. Let's plan on getting together in three months, and let's plan on doing a complete history and physical at that time.

Please tell Sarah, my receptionist at the front, that you need an early morning appointment for a history and physical. It takes about an hour or more. Don't eat anything after dinner the night before."

"I am going to recommend that you see Dr. Aaron Jones about this problem with your biopsy. He's an excellent surgeon."

"I'm sure he is," said Linda. But privately she was thinking, *I know people at the hospital who can give us a second opinion about Dr. Jones. I want to check him out before we make a commitment.*

Dr. Smith knew that Linda didn't accept medical recommendations on blind faith. As the caretaker of her family, she would do her own 'due diligence' on Dr. Jones or any other physician Dr. Smith referred. He knew that if she had questions or concerns, he would be consulted. In an odd way, he respected Linda's desire to take responsibility. Doctors who thought of themselves as gods, unwilling to consider their patient's point of view, are an endangered species, and he wasn't about to become one of them.

"Well, Mrs. Chance, let me know what you and Tom decide. Then I'll have Cindy arrange an appointment."

"Thanks, Dr. Smith. We appreciate your meeting with us," said Linda.

Tom nodded and shook his hand. "Thanks, Doc. I'll see you again in about three months." As a seasoned sales representative, Tom knew how to maintain composure and project confidence, but inside he was shaken. God, he thought, I'm only 43. I thought you didn't have to worry about cancer until you were older.

Linda took his arm and together they left Dr. Smith's office. Tom did not remember his father having any skin cancer, but then he died when he was only 54 years old from a heart attack. Tom still missed him, especially at times like these when he wished he could just talk to him for a little while. Tom didn't really understand his father very well until after he and Linda had their first child. *We live life forward, and understand it backwards,* he thought. *We always want to grow up in a hurry, and then wish the clock would slow down.*

Linda took Tom's hand and gave it a loving squeeze. "I'm sure it's going to be OK, Tom. Let's just get some pizza for dinner. We'll talk to Cindy and set things up with a plastic surgeon in a few days."

"Yeah. Fine."

LESSON SIX

The insurance company is not the enemy. The government is not the enemy. The bureaucracy is not the enemy. A bad relationship or a bad outcome with a physician or a hospital is not the enemy. The disease is the enemy. Do not lose your focus on what you are fighting and what you are fighting for.

CHAPTER 7

The Foundation

"The height of the wall depends on the depth of the foundation."

– Chinese Proverb

Tom called from his cell phone on his way home from the office. It was just past 6:00, and the traffic, as usual, was slow. "Linda, I'm running a little late. Michael has a meeting with the Chess Club at 7:00. I can still take him, but if you could go ahead and set dinner out it'll help. I need to eat and run."

"No problem. Where are you?" she asked.

"On my way home."

"OK. By the way, Cindy was able to set up the appointment with Dr. Jones this Wednesday.

"Oh, boy, I can hardly wait." Tom was beginning to feel like some "thing" that was scheduled without his knowledge or consent. It was irritating. But they had agreed that Linda would make the arrangements.

"Don't be difficult, Tom. *And don't even think about conflicts at work.* It's not easy getting these appointments with specialists."

"Yeah, I know. See you in about 10 minutes." Tom clicked off the phone. His throat felt dry. *All these doctors' appointments wear on my nerves,* he thought.

Tonight the members were playing chess in quads, with each player assigned to each of the other three opponents in thirty-minute games. Michael was matched with Dr. Kong's grandson.

"Good evening." Tom said sitting down next to Dr. Kong.

"Yes, it is a good evening." Dr. Kong nodded and noticed the book, *Living With Cancer,* in Tom's hand. "I see the kite has been rising," he said, motioning at the book.

It took Tom a moment to understand. He wasn't sure if it was a statement or a question. "Yes. Well, you know that little mole I had taken off by Dr. Smith turned out to be skin cancer. So I'm trying to read up a little on it and, you know, trying to understand my options, but I'm having a hard time.

"How so?" Dr. Kong asked.

"Well, I ordered this book over the Internet, but it seems to be written for people suffering from–how would you say it?–a more advanced form of the disease."

"It is not always necessary to dive to the bottom of the ocean to find seashells," said Dr. Kong.

"Grandfather, we are getting ready to start! Do you have any last words of advice?" asked An-Huan.

"The skillful commander first creates a strong defense, then watches for weakness in his opponent. This is a teaching of Sun-tzu; remember it and you will do well."

Turning back to Tom, Dr. Kong said, "I apologize for my grandson. The mind learns best when the heart opens. And I am sorry to hear this news from Dr. Smith."

"It's no big deal," Tom said casually, then thought, *maybe it is*. It's just that, well ... I've always enjoyed good health. And now this!"

"You do not have control ..."

"At least I've got a doctor now, but I'm not sure how to work with him. I feel almost like I need a coach ... to help me, you know, learn how to work with him."

"So you wish to learn medical strategy and tactics from the *patient's* point of view, rather than from the physician's point of view?"

Tom looked at Dr. Kong intently. "You know, I never really thought of it that way before, but I think you're right. I want to know how to deal with the medical system so I can get the best possible care." Tom looked away. The memories of his father and now Bill made him feel vulnerable for the first time in years. "My dad died in his mid-fifties, and just recently a good friend my age died of a heart attack. I want to live a longer life. After all, nobody looks after you better than yourself. Right?"

"Perhaps, Mr. Chance. Although I know men whose wives take better care of them than they do themselves," Dr. Kong replied. He realized that Tom now needed an advocate, and conversation here at the chess club would be difficult at best.

"Let me make a suggestion, Mr. Chance. The children are occupied with their games and we are not allowed to provide advice tonight, so perhaps you and I could go to the coffee and tea shop across the street where we could continue our conversation without being interrupted."

The offer was unexpected, but to Tom it seemed like a life buoy tossed to him in a deep, dark sea. "Thanks, Dr. Kong. That would be great," Tom said gratefully.

"How do you say, "Don't give it a second thought?'" Dr. Kong smiled to relieve the tension. Inwardly he congratulated himself for this time having a Western catch phrase to offer.

A few customers were reading newspapers in the coffee shop. Soft, instrumental music played in the background, creating a relaxed mood.

"How can I help you, gentlemen?" the waitress asked.

"I'll take a cappuccino, please," said Tom.

"Do you have green tea?" asked Dr. Kong.

"Yes, we just started serving it. Seems to be kind of a hot item, especially in New York and on the West Coast.

"Thank you," said Dr. Kong.

Dr. Kong and Tom found a quiet corner where they would not disturb the other customers.

"Now, Mr. Chance, where were we?"

"You were asking if I would like to understand medical strategy better from the patient's perspective."

"Yes, let us start with fundamental concepts and key principles. First, the height of the wall depends on the depth of the foundation."

"I'm sorry, Dr. Kong, but I don't follow."

"In order for you to achieve longevity and happiness, you must first come to understand the nature of the enemy and have realistic expectations. Once there was a farmer who wished to buy the perfect horse. Every morning he would go to the markets looking for the perfect horse until one day a gentleman stopped him, and asked what type of horse he would like to buy. Bowing deeply before the gentleman, he answered, "For me, sir, there is only one perfect horse. A horse that does not eat grass."

Tom smiled at the story. He understood what Dr. Kong was saying. A reasonable person should not expect to live forever. No argument. But what is a reasonable expectation? Shouldn't I strive to live longer than my father before me? Shouldn't I hope to live at least to the average life expectancy for men in this country? Hadn't this venerable Asian man exceeded that average? "Tell me, Dr. Kong, is there a maximum life expectancy?" he asked

"Every one is born with a different, but immeasurable capacity for longevity. So the maximum height of the wall varies. Also, the depth of the foundation necessary to reach that height varies. Who can predict when the enemy will attack? A thief comes in the night. Sun-tzu says, 'Do not hope on your enemy not coming, but depend on yourself being prepared.' For this reason, first focus on digging the foundation, then build the wall with diligence.

"Value quality of life as much as quantity of life. Let the arrow fall neither short nor far. Aim true to your target. To achieve longevity and happiness you must understand the nature and the character of your opponent. No one can defeat an unknown enemy."

"But with so many diseases, Dr. Kong, how could a lay person understand them? It would be too overwhelming," said Tom.

"The patient should understand strategy; let the physician recommend tactics. Medicine has thousands of tactics against disease, but the patient should understand fundamental strategy. A wise general knows the structure of his opponent's army, even though he wins the battle soldier by soldier.

"Understand the two ways, the way of nature and the way of man. All things, living and nonliving, tend to randomness and disorder, but in their own time. A law of nature commands it. For this reason, every disease has an element of time. If the patient and the physician interrupt the process in time, then the conflict can be won, and the person lives. This principle was discovered thousands of years ago by the physician Hippocrates" Dr. Kong fixed his gaze out the window as he recited from memory the ancient words of the father of western medicine:

> Life is short; the art of medicine long; opportunity fleeting; experience deceptive; judgment difficult. The physician must not only care for the patient, but must also secure the cooperation of the sick, of those in attendance, and of all the external agents.

Looking back at Tom, Dr. Kong asked, "Have you ever wondered why physicians do not charge for phone calls? They know opportunity can be fleeting. Their success depends upon the patient giving them sufficient time to intervene. Without opportunity, ability has no value."

"I see," said Tom, "but what is 'the way of man.'"

"The way of man overcomes the way of nature. Man uses the mind and creates tools, but most importantly, man uses relationships. At the heart of healing stands a relationship."

"You lost me again, Dr. Kong."

"Example teaches better than principle. Why did you go see Dr. Smith about this mole?" asked Dr. Kong.

"Well, I was worried about it. No. Wait a minute. That's not true. Actually, I didn't want to see Dr. Smith about it. I guess I was denying that it could be a problem, but Linda, my wife, kept insisting that I get it checked out and finally I was so tired of her persistence that I kept the appointment." Tom felt a little uncomfortable. The insight did not make him feel very proud of himself.

"Your wife does well. Determination and misfortune are old enemies," said Dr. Kong.

"So you're saying my relationship with my wife – something you call 'the way of man' – is actually part of my medical care?" asked Tom a little puzzled.

"Yes. Your relationship with your wife provided your relationship with your physician the opportunity. The physician then uses his skill to analyze and develop the plan to attack the disease and temporarily defeat the way of nature. Without either relationship, the window of opportunity might have closed before you saw a knowledgeable physician."

"Let's hope you're right," Tom sighed.

"Of course, Mr. Chance, I presume much."

"Please, call me Tom."

"I have not seen the pathology report, so I do not know if the window has already closed. Names are also very important."

Dr. Kong glanced at his watch, "It is getting late, and we need to get back to the library. Perhaps we can talk further this next weekend. You have much to learn. The chess club plays in a tournament in Bethesda, Maryland this weekend. An-Huan will be playing. Is Michael coming also?"

"Sure. We'll be there. I would like to talk some more."

As they walked back toward the library, Tom thought to himself, *I wonder what he means by 'names are also important.'* He wasn't sure, but he knew Dr. Kong was teaching him something that most people never understood. "You know, thanks for talking with me, Dr. Kong. I have a hard time talking about medical things, even with Linda. Somehow, just talking makes me feel better about things."

"You are welcome, Mr., uh, Tom. My ancestors gave the Kong family much knowledge and wisdom. I carry this tradition within me. We will talk again this weekend. May your years grow as high as the mountains, and your heart be as peaceful as still waters."

"Hey, where were you, dad? I thought I had An-Huan in a draw when he surprised me at the end by advancing a pawn; but instead of becoming a queen, he promoted the pawn to a knight for an immediate checkmate. That guy plays great chess!"

"Yes, he is member of the Kong family," Tom replied with new respect.

"What does that have to do with anything, dad?" Michael looked up at his father puzzled.

"Sometimes your family has to do with everything, son. Let's go. We promised your mom we'd be home by 10:00."

As he lay in bed Tom could not get the conversation with Dr. Kong out of his mind. *"The way of man overcomes the way of nature. All things, living and nonliving, tend to randomness and disorder, but in their own time." Time. "Man uses the mind, creates tools, but most importantly, uses relationships. At the heart of healing stands a relationship."* Looking over at Linda he noticed she had already gone to sleep. He kissed her gently on the forehead. "Thanks, honey," then turning over he made a mental note before falling asleep: *remember to send Dr. Smith a thank-you note in the morning*. The love of his wife had brought him to the doctor, but the skill and diligence of his physician lay at the heart of his hope for healing.

LESSON SEVEN

Everyone is born with a different capacity for health and longevity, but your ability to reach your potential depends on how well you lay down the foundation for a long life: a healthy diet and regular exercise combined with avoiding high risk behaviors dig a deep foundation to reaching your maximum life expectancy. (See **www.drpen.com/dietandexercise** & **www.drpen.com/highriskbehavior**)

CHAPTER 8

Friend or Foe

"If you are patient in one moment of anger, you will escape a hundred days of sorrow."

—Chinese Proverb

I understand how time and chance characterize disease, Tom thought to himself, *but I wonder what he means by 'names are also important.'* Tom walked into the waiting room to see Dr. Aaron Jones, the plastic surgeon. The waiting room felt cold, unfriendly and crowded. Modern paintings with harsh colors decorated the walls. An elderly woman, without smiling or greeting him, handed him a clipboard of papers for him to fill out. He felt out of place and unwelcome.

Before he could finish the forms a nurse came out and called him. "Mr. Chance, come with me. You can bring those forms with you and fill them out in the exam room."

She put him in a small room and closed the door behind her. He could hear people moving outside the door occasionally. After 30 minutes or so he began to wonder if they had forgotten him. The room was cold. The nurse had asked him to get undressed with only a disposable paper gown to wear. He was starting to get a little angry when a tall, thin man looking down at a chart walked into the room followed by a young woman dressed in a short white lab coat. Tom recognized her as the medical student from the night when Bill had died, but she didn't recognize him. She seemed much more detached and cool and failed to introduce herself or why she was even there. *I guess she's getting toughened up a bit,* Tom thought to himself.

"So you're the malignant melanoma?" the man asked without looking up.

Tom wasn't sure to how to answer. "Dr. Smith referred me to you," he said.

"Right. He sent me the path report. Well, this is a pretty cut and dried case. We're going to need to do a wider excision. I'll see if we can't get it on the schedule for early next week. My nurse will explain the procedure to you, and we'll need you to sign some forms to let us do the surgery. OK?"

Before Tom could ask any questions, the man left the room. He could hear the doctor explaining the case to the medical student outside the door. Tom felt cheated. *I've been waiting in here for almost an hour and this guy didn't even look at me.* He didn't know what to do, so he got dressed and waited. After another 20 minutes the nurse came back in and handed him a pamphlet explaining the procedure and some forms he needed to complete and bring with him to the hospital.

"Unless you sign these forms Dr. Jones can't do the operation, so be sure you bring them to the hospital the day of your surgery."

"OK." Tom said, but inwardly he wondered why he had to go to the hospital. He thought the doctor was just going to do it right here in the office today. But he kept his thoughts to himself. He knew he needed to get this done, and he knew from his conversation with Dr. Kong time was important. Still, something felt wrong. He could not put it into words, but in his heart he could sense danger.

When he arrived back home he tried to talk to Linda about it. "I don't know, Linda. Something just doesn't seem right. This doctor never looked me in the eye. He never even called me by my name. He said, 'So you're the malignant something or other.'"

"Now, Tom, calm down. I talked to at least four people at the hospital, including two doctors, and they all gave Dr. Jones high marks."

"I'll bet it wasn't from Charm School," Tom grumbled.

"Maybe that's why he's a surgeon," Linda offered. "When you're out cold and under the knife, charm isn't very important. But if Dr. Smith referred him to you, I'm sure he does good work. Besides, you saw his profile from the Board of Medicine. Excellent credentials."

"What a cold fish! He didn't even give me a chance to ask any questions. He just had his nurse throw a brochure at me and tell me to sign a bunch of papers or he's not going to do the procedure. Maybe I don't want him doing the procedure anyway!"

"Tom, let's sleep on it a couple of days and not do anything rash. OK? If you don't feel different by Monday, I'll talk to Dr. Smith. In the meantime, I'll try to look over some of the papers for you. I know all this medical stuff makes it hard for you to concentrate on your work."

"OK, thanks. I guess I'm just edgy about this thing." He wanted to change the subject. "How's Michael doing in school? We're supposed to go up to Bethesda this weekend for a regional chess tournament. He really likes the library chess club. I think he's making some good friends. This boy, An-Huan, is really smart."

"You know, Tom, I thought chess would distract him from his school work, but actually he seems to be doing better. His teachers have noticed a difference, too. His math teacher just laughed when I told her. She said, 'They're all like that in the school chess club. It's good for them.' I'm beginning to believe her."

Tom thought for a moment and answered, "I think it has a lot to do with the game."

"How so?"

"Well, chess developed as a war game, but it maintains the cultural ethics of a sport. In chess you don't try to kill the opponent's men, you capture them. It's not like these video games with realistic graphics and violence. Right now, Michael is learning tactical chess. Later, as he advances and matures, his coach will emphasize strategy and positional play."

"Whatever you say, Tom. I don't even know how to play it. But to answer your question, yes, he's doing well in school."

"Speaking of that, did you read the email from Sarah? Sounds like she's doing well, too."

"Uh-huh. I just hope we did the right thing, letting her go away to school."

Tom knew this was Linda's way of saying, *I miss my daughter.* And he did too when he let himself think about it. When Sarah first applied to Brown University, he thought, *why so far away?* He wondered if even Dr. Kong had a proverb that would explain it.

Tom calmed down over the next couple of days, and by the time the weekend arrived he had almost decided to go ahead and let Dr. Jones do the surgery and get it over with.

LESSON EIGHT

Understand what your goals are in professional relationships. In this age of exploding medical knowledge and specialization, be sure to understand what you are trying to accomplish in the relationship and that your expectations are based on your goals. Insist on being treated with respect! Have courage! If you are not accomplishing your goals in a professional relationship, then discuss this with your doctor, your nurse, and/or your caregiver(s) and decide whether you need to make a change. (See also the Agency for Healthcare Research and Quality's Questions to Ask Before Having Surgery at **http://www.ahrq.gov/consumer/surgery.htm)**

CHAPTER 9

The Living Ancestor

"When the character of a man is not clear to you, look at his friends."

—Japanese Proverb

"How are you ranked in the tournament?" Tom asked Michael.

"Around 1200. But if I do well, I could move up 100 or 200 points."

Tom thought he was being overly optimistic, but didn't say anything. They were on the road headed to the regional chess tournament in Bethesda. It was one of those times when Tom found it easy to have long conversations with Michael . . . when he would willingly engage in father-son chit-chat.

"Is An-Huan coming?"

"Yeah, we're on the same team. You know, Dad, he was telling me his grandfather had to have surgery last week."

"Oh. I'm sorry to hear that. Is he doing OK?" Tom asked, surprised.

"Well, he said it was no big deal. Apparently he goes to a skin specialist every six months and usually has to have something done every time he goes."

"What does he have done?" Tom asked.

"I don't know. Huan never said." *So Dr. Kong has 'skin problems' too,* Tom thought. Interesting.

"Did you know Dr. Kong just turned 79 years old!" Michael emphasized the age as if it belonged in the Guiness Book of Records. "He sure doesn't look it."

"It's hard to tell with someone like Dr. Kong," Tom answered.

Michael was now full of information. "Huan says he grew up in China. Someplace called Qufu. It's kind of interesting. There's a famous mountain nearby called, I think, Taishan that his grandfather used to climb as a boy. The legend says that if a person climbs Taishan he will live to be a 100 years old," Michael said in a hushed voice, as if he half believed it.

"Wow," Tom replied, lifting his eyebrows, pretending amazement. Michael didn't seem to notice.

"Yeah. He came to the United States in his mid-twenties to study medicine, but because of the wars he couldn't go back. What war was that, dad?"

"It was the Chinese Civil War when the Communist Party seized control of China after the Second World War. Millions of Chinese were killed or driven off the mainland."

"Anyway, when the war started, his family warned him to remain in America. And his brother had to flee to Taiwan! Most of his family lives in Taiwan now, although some live in Hong Kong and a few are in Canada. Some are starting to return to Qufu, but not many."

"Really!"

"That's not all, dad. His older brother died three years ago and now Huan's grandfather is the *oldest relative* to carry the Kong family name. In the Kong family, they call the oldest male relative 'the living ancestor.'"

"So, you mean, Dr. Kong is now the Kong family's living ancestor?"

"That's right! Not only is he the living ancestor, he is so healthy that many in his family believe he will live 115 years. None of the previous living ancestors has lived that long for over a 1000 years!"

Tom thought to himself, *I wonder how much of this is legend and how much is fact? The way he speaks, though, in sayings and parables, almost seems like he's from a different time.*

"Well, Michael, we're here. The parking lot's pretty full. I didn't realize these tournaments were so large."

Tom and Michael exited the car and started walking toward the conference center. "Look, Dad. There's Huan and his grandfather over there. Let's go meet them." Michael ran ahead and Tom quickened his pace.

"Good morning, Dr. Kong. Hi, An-Huan. It's a beautiful day," Tom greeted them.

"Good morning, Mr. Chance. Good morning, Michael. Success favors the diligent. Are you ready for the tournament?" asked Dr. Kong.

"Yes, sir. An-Huan and I have been studying the classic openings, and I have made improvements in my end-game."

"Good. From knowledge comes strength. Both you and An-Huan record your games. We will analyze them later. They are very strict about the rules here so we will not be able to discuss them until after the tournament. Let's see where you have been placed."

They went into the large conference hall where Huan and Michael found their seats and began to play.

Turning to Tom, Dr. Kong asked, "Mr. Chance, I noticed an out-door cafe close by. Would you like to go there while the boys play? The tournament will last a few hours, break for lunch, and then finish this afternoon."

"Sure."

After ordering coffee and tea, Dr. Kong and Tom sat at a small table on the sidewalk. Tom relaxed and felt the warm autumn sun on his back.

"I see you have not had this place removed on your neck," began Dr. Kong.

"I went to see the surgeon on Wednesday. He scheduled me for out-patient surgery this Tuesday morning."

"I see."

Tom hesitated for a moment, then decided he would confess his feelings about Dr. Jones. He had been planning it for days.

"You know, Dr. Kong, actually I felt a little uncomfortable with him. He treated me more like a disease than a person. Maybe I shouldn't complain. My wife says he has an excellent reputation."

"Zhang-Yu says, 'Compete for alliances or risk isolation with little help.'"

"Who is Zhang-Yu?"

"Zhang-Yu is a famous disciple of Sun-tzu."

"Uhh . . . I'm sorry Dr. Kong, but I'm not familiar with these people. Who is Sun-tzu?"

"Sun-tzu is the greatest military strategist China ever produced. He was a student of the Way and he lived a few hundred years after the famous ancestor of the Kong family. Like the waters of a natural lake, the wisdom of China wells up from many sources. Now, I wanted to teach you the importance of names today, but the enemy moves fast. Ideally, the best time to chose a physician is when you are well. We will speak of names another day. Today, we speak of alliances."

"I guess Americans kind of pride themselves on being independent, Dr. Kong. I don't really go out trying to make alliances with people. My relationships just kind of develop spontaneously. I certainly don't go out trying to make friends with doctors just because I might need them one day. It would make me feel kind of calculating, like I was using people for my own selfish gain."

"Mr. Chance, I know you do not know the Kong family, but the saying of negative reciprocity comes from my ancestor, Confucius: 'Do *not* do unto others what you would not have them do unto you.' A moral code underlies all relationships. Loyalty and faithfulness cannot be seen. The reason we are here today, chess, provides an example."

Tom leaned forward to listen carefully, knowing that any lesson would have to be extracted from the analogy Dr. Kong delivered. He would have preferred a straight-forward explanation, but he knew that was not the teaching style of 'living ancestors.'

"Which is the most valuable piece in chess?"

"Well, the queen. She can move in any direction," Tom answered.

"No. The queen is the most powerful, but she is not the most valuable. The king is the most valuable. Lose your queen and the game continues; lose your king and the game ends. The relationships between the king and his pieces determine who will prevail. Power must be understood in relationships for the way of man to defeat the way of nature. Even the most knowledgeable and skillful physician in the world cannot defend himself against disease unless a relationship with another physician assists him. Professional relationships determine success. Ignore them with peril. The seamstress does not weave the cloth from a single thread. A builder does not build the wall with a single stone," Dr. Kong replied forcefully.

"OK. I'm sorry. I guess I was being a little naïve," Tom said. He felt a little warm after drinking his coffee and took off his jacket. "I've always avoided doctors as much as possible, just like my father.

I don't think he ever saw a doctor until the day he died." Tom would always remember that day as a 10-year-old standing outside the emergency room at Saint Bernadine's Hospital engulfed in sadness and grief. *He can't be dead,* he remembered saying to himself over and over, *I was just throwing a baseball with him yesterday.* He felt the wound reopen deep in his heart. He never wanted that to happen to Michael.

"I guess I've always been afraid of what they would say to me," he said looking up at Dr. Kong. "It hurt a lot when I lost my dad."

"The loss of a father wounds deeply, but remember the principle we discussed last week: 'Do not hope on your enemy not coming, but depend on yourself being prepared.' Disease attacks you; disease cannot directly attack the alliance. Do not allow the disease to weaken the alliance by creating doubt and confusion. Do not let well-meaning friends or family weaken the alliance. At the heart of healing stands a relationship – the patient-physician relationship."

"That's all well and good, Dr. Kong." Tom didn't want to surrender his position without a fight. "But this doctor I saw two days ago was ... a jerk. I'm not sure I trust him. I feel like I never connected with him. He made me feel like I was the disease; in fact he didn't even call me by my name. He said, 'So you're the malignant something or other.' It didn't feel like much of a relationship to me."

"Where does the value lie in the relationship?" asked Dr. Kong.

"In the doctor, of course. I don't know how to do surgery and I certainly can't do it on myself," Tom answered feeling a little flustered.

"The queen is the most powerful piece in chess, but she is not the most valuable."

Tom felt like he had a headache. He was not used to continually thinking in analogies.

"The patient has the power to say *yes;* the patient has the power to say *no.* If the patient does not provide the opportunity, the surgeon's skill has no value."

"But how would I know if it is safe to say *no* and look for another physician?"

"Do not draw the bow and not release the arrow. You must know the nature of the enemy and the nature of the attack. No one can effectively fight a nameless adversary. You will learn how to determine this later, but for now you must learn how to choose a physician properly. If you want to cross the river, build a bridge. The patient in the patient-physician relationship should aim to create an *effective healing alliance.* To achieve this goal you must evaluate the physician's character, competence, and communication skills."

"Well, I've already evaluated this doctor's communication skills ... zero!"

"First, determine character. Is he willing to serve you? Will he put your interests above his own? People who know the physician, but are not his personal advocates, best answer these questions. Ask former patients, office staff, and nurses who have worked with him.

"Second, determine competence. Do other physicians and nurses recommend him? Does your primary-care physician recommend him? Is he board certified? How many years of experience does he have? How many of these procedures has he done? Are there any problems with the state licensing board? Keep these questions in balance. Age and experience support judgment; youth and proximity to training often indicate superior technical ability."

"Third, determine communication skills. Does he meet your eye when talking with you? Does he give you the opportunity to explain your symptoms without interruptions? Does he explain his assessment in terms you can understand? Does he propose a plan or does he mandate one? Does he allow you time to ask questions?"

"Well, Linda says he is an excellent surgeon, and he takes good care of his patients, but ..."

"Why did Dr. Smith recommend him?" asked Dr. Kong.

"I don't know," answered Tom.

"Whenever one ally recommends another, the motives must be examined."

"What difference does it make, Dr. Kong? I thought he mainly had to recommend someone who participates in my insurance plan."

Dr. Kong explained that insurance plans were a secondary ally in making medical choices. Insurance companies and plans often influence the patient's choice of the first ally, the primary care physician, and it is important to understand the relationship between these entities. Today, insurance companies often limit the number of allies at the patient's disposal, perhaps for the better since insurers formally evaluate medical competency. But a poor ally could sacrifice competence for price, so patients must be careful. "Prudence is the vehicle of a long journey. Choices remain."

"Well, I think Dr. Smith and Dr. Jones are in the same group, the Templeton Clinic."

"Then Dr. Smith has a bias to refer patients to specialists within his own group."

"I guess he does."

"Then conflicts of interest may arise, but again keep the questions in balance. Multi-specialty groups often have a more rigorous evaluation process in choosing partners than single-specialty groups, but you should be aware of the bias in case you, as the patient, need to overrule. In complex or higher risk cases, the primary-care physician brings the specialist physician, the third ally, into the battle. He is a powerful piece and wields tactics that can do good as well as cause harm. You and your primary physician must weigh the risks and benefits and use specialists appropriately.

You think I'm placing too much importance on Dr. Jones's personality–or lack thereof?"

"Aim for the right care at the right place at the right time. In this case, you believe that Dr. Jones serves his patients well and is a competent surgeon. He does not communicate well, but you primarily need a procedure from him and not a long-term relationship. Time would suggest it is best to proceed. 'We are not trying to buy a horse that doesn't eat grass.'

"It is getting close to lunchtime, and we should go back to meet the boys. Would you and Michael like to join us for lunch? The Hunan Chef serves excellent food."

"Great. We don't have any plans."

When they entered the conference hall, Michael and An-Huan ran up to them. "We did pretty good, dad. I won one game, lost one game, and had to stalemate the last game. An-Huan won two games, and was forced to draw the last game by a perpetual check."

"That's great. Dr. Kong invited us to go with them to a Chinese restaurant. Would you like to go?"

"Sure. Come on, An-Huan. Let's get our stuff. We only have about an hour before the afternoon games."

Tom asked Dr. Kong to order for them, as he was unfamiliar with the names. The conversation centered on the boys who were very excited about how well they had done that morning.

"Dr. Kong. Did you used to play competitive chess?" asked Michael.

"Yes, many years ago. In China, we often played chess outdoors in the evenings. We call it 'catching the breeze' when it is too hot to stay indoors. I have fond memories of warm summer nights playing with my brothers and sisters."

"But did you ever play here in the States?"

"Yes, in college. I played for the team at Columbia University in New York. We had a Russian coach who defected from the Soviet Union."

"Did you win?"

"Yes. Our team did well, but we did not win the championship."

"That's too bad."

"The dark horse learns lessons the champion never perceives,"

Dr. Kong replied.

"Let's finish up boys. We need to get back to the tournament in 15 minutes," Tom interrupted. After paying they walked out to the parking lot. "I understand you have had skin surgery recently, Dr. Kong. Huan told Michael."

"Yes, too much sun as a boy in Qingdao."

"I see. What surgeon do you use?"

Turning slightly with a whimsical smile, he answered, "Dr. Jones. Once the diagnosis becomes clear, skillful action, not words, determine success with surgeons."

LESSON NINE

Base your choice of a physician on character, competence, and communication skills. Friends and family can give valuable input on character and communication skills, but you should rely on the recommendations of other heath professionals and the physician's certification accomplishments to determine competence.

CHAPTER 10

The Window of Opportunity

After the afternoon sessions were under way Dr. Kong and Tom returned to the coffee and tea shop. Tom felt sleepy. Dr. Kong's stamina amazed him. In fact, the conversation seemed to invigorate him. *He was born to teach,* Tom thought to himself.

"Now, Mr. Chance – I'm sorry, Tom – where were we? I believe we have discussed the proper methods to follow in choosing allies, correct?"

"Yes. We discussed a way to evaluate physicians," Tom answered.

"Rivers have two shores, and relationships have two sides. To build a bridge to cross a river, you build from both sides," Dr. Kong began.

"I guess I'm a little sleepy after lunch. I'm not following you, again."

"Remember, the patient establishes the patient-physician relationship to create an *effective healing alliance.* Every relationship has two sides. We have discussed ways of choosing your allies based on character, competency, and communication skills while being cautious of competing motives that can undermine the effectiveness of the relationship. Professional ethics codes, such as the American Medical Association Principles of Medical Ethics and the American Hospital Association Patient's Bill of Rights as well as other ethical and legal codes, clearly outline the rights and responsibilities of health care providers and patients. Legislation, however, does not determine the *effectiveness* of the relationship."

"The mission of the patient-physician relationship remains constant. Doctors work to discover what is wrong and strive to help the patient without causing harm. But to be effective the physician needs the patient to tell him what is wrong. Six out of ten times the physician discovers what is wrong from the patient's history of the problem, two out of ten times the physician discovers what is wrong from the patient's physical examination, and one out of ten times the physician discovers what is wrong from the patient's laboratory studies and diagnostic tests."

"I see," said Tom, but mentally questioning why this doesn't add up to ten. "Even if I chose a great physician, it doesn't really help me if he can't discover what's wrong, and you're saying it's the *patient* who primarily helps the physician discover it!"

"Exactly, Tom. First, the patient must seek the physician's help before the window of opportunity closes. Second, the patient must cooperate with the physician. Recall the principle discovered by Hypocrites thousands of years ago: 'Life is short; the art is long; opportunity fleeting; experience deceptive; judgment difficult. It is the duty of the physician not only to care for the patient but also to secure the cooperation of the sick, of those in attendance, and of all the external agents.' The physician may also discover the truth when he secures the cooperation of the sick and the cooperation of the patient's family and friends. Strength or power may determine temporary gain or loss, but devotion to truth determines long-term victory or defeat. The patient must be open and honest with his physician. Likewise, the physician must be open and truthful with the patient. Eloquence persuades, but honesty buys loyalty."

"I think most patients try to be honest with their doctors," said Tom.

"Perception differs from experience. Without telling their doctor, as many as 50% of patients with high blood pressure never take their medications within one year of their physician's prescription. Less than 20% of patients alter their lifestyle despite recommendations from the physician."

"Well, you know, sometimes it's hard to take a medication four times a day – they're expensive, and it's difficult to find time to exercise and eat right," Tom replied defensively.

"Small drops become a great river. Patients do not follow their physicians' advice for many reasons. The physician and the patient can address these tactically by prescribing or requesting medications with simple dosing schedules and using calendars, pillboxes and other devices. They can negotiate honest compromises. Most importantly, however, when the patient-physician relationship lacks conviction and commitment, patients don't follow their physicians' advice, even when they trust the physician's character and competence. Often this occurs because patients do not understand how physicians work, or they do not trust how the doctor came to his conclusions."

Taking out a pen Dr. Kong wrote on the back of his napkin: *Physicians create a* **MAP** *to take patients from their current condition to an improved condition.*

Physicians:
<u>M</u>ake inquiries and examinations
<u>A</u>ssess the problem
<u>P</u>rescribe a treatment

"Physicians do one or all three of these activities with every patient encounter," Dr. Kong said as he put his pen back in his pocket.

Tom picked up the napkin and studied it. "OK, I understand *what* they're doing, but I don't understand *how* they do this work," said Tom looking up at Dr. Kong.

"The better the patient understands this process, the better the patient will help the physician discover what is wrong. Remember, six out of ten times the physician discovers what is wrong from talking with the patient. The better the patient communicates with the physician, the better the physician understands the problem, and the more accurately the physician prescribes treatment. The archer does not bend the bow until he sees the target."

"But *how* do physicians see the target?" asked Tom intrigued. He had never thought about the actual process physicians go through to diagnose a patient's illness. He had always assumed it was too complicated to understand, but Dr. Kong had a way of making it understandable and not so intimidating.

"Physicians organize information in a very specific way. They first want to know the patient's greatest concern. They call this the 'chief complaint.' A patient who spends five to ten minutes before the visit with their physician listing and *prioritizing* their concerns goes a long way toward helping their physician better understand their problem. Next, the physician determines the 'history of the present illness.' Here the physician pieces together the patient's story. How did the problem develop over time? Communication flows two ways. The patient tells the story in his own words for one or two minutes. The physician asks questions to clarify his understanding.

The physician also needs to know relevant medical information from the patient's past, the current medications the patient is taking, and any allergies to medications. One of my ancestors wrote, 'The best memory falls inferior to even a marginal written record.' The Kong family archives are over 2000 years old and are renowned in China. A patient saves both the physician and himself a tremendous amount of time by keeping written records of his previous medical problems, current medications, and allergies to medications. This allows the physician to focus on the current problem. At times he may need to explore the social and family history. If the patient has a long-standing relationship with the physician, this information is usually gathered during a preventive complete history and physical and not repeated in the middle of an acute illness. The physician keeps this information in his charts. A long-term relationship with the same physician tends to produce better outcomes. The patient trusts the physician, the assessment convinces the patient, and the patient commits to the treatment plan. Finally, the physician asks questions reviewing all the major organ systems, then performs a physical examination." Dr. Kong took a sip of tea.

"OK, so what I need to write down and then prioritize are my major concerns. Should I limit them to just two or three?" asked Tom.

"Yes, prioritize the top three, but write them all down and just give them to the physician. What may not seem important to you may be important to him."

"OK, and then I should keep a list of any medical problems I have had in the past, a list of my medications, and any allergies?"

"Yes, this is sufficient. A patient with a serious, chronic illness with multiple allies may need to do more, but every patient should keep these three essential records in his wallet or pocketbook."

"Thank you, Dr. Kong. I never understood how I should or even could work better with my physician."

"You are welcome. The boys should be finishing soon. I think we should return to the convention hall." Dr. Kong stood up.

"Right." Tom left a tip on the table and they walked back to the convention hall. *It makes sense,* Tom thought to himself. *If I can tell the physician the one thing that bothers me the most, it should provide him with the strongest lead to the problem."*

Tom picked at the back of his neck. He was looking forward to getting the biopsy site removed. He glanced over at Dr. Kong. *I guess the bow is drawn. I hope this surgeon aims well.*

LESSON TEN

When you go to your doctor, WRITE down all of your concerns and problems on a piece of paper. Give this piece of paper or a copy to your doctor, but be sure to underline or circle the one problem that you are the most worried about. (Also see, **www.drpen.com/doctorvisit**)

CHAPTER 11

Surgery

"Tom Chance," the receptionist called out in the crowded hospital waiting room.

"Yes," Tom answered. He had a slight headache from fasting overnight.

"Please come to the registration desk at booth four."

Tom found the desk where an elderly woman with gray hair and reading glasses was busily entering data into a computer.

"Good morning," Tom ventured.

"Good morning. Please take a seat. I will be with you in a moment." After a few moments the woman asked, "Are you Thomas Chance?"

"Yes. I'm scheduled for surgery with Dr. Jones."

"Yes. Have you ever been a patient at this hospital before?"

"No."

"Since you are not on our pre-registration list, we will need you to fill out some forms for us. Please fill these out and bring them back to me. We are required by law to inform you about your rights under the Natural Death Act. If something happens to you while you are in the hospital and you become incapacitated, we need to know if you would want us to give you artificial life support. Please take this brochure and fill out the form for the Natural Death Act on the bottom as well as the form to designate a Health Care Power of Attorney if you do not already have one." She handed him a brochure explaining the Natural Death Act along with a clipboard full of forms.

"Thank you," Tom answered. He thought, *maybe I should have had Linda stay with me instead of coming back after taking Michael to school. I thought this was going to be a fairly simple procedure.*

Tom filled out the forms, returned them to the woman and waited.

"Mr. Chance?"

"Yes," Tom looked up at a young man dressed in white, pushing a wheelchair.

"I'm Jerry with transportation. I'm going to take you to the outpatient surgery center. I just need to check your wristband first. Thanks. Now, take a seat."

"Why do I need to go in a wheelchair? I'm perfectly capable of walking," Tom protested.

"Hospital policy," the attendant shrugged.

Tom didn't want to make a scene, so he got into the wheelchair feeling a little less like a person and more like a part on an assembly line. He tried to engage the attendant in a conversation, but within a few minutes they had arrived.

"Mr. Chance? Good morning, I'm Eileen. I'm going to be your nurse today."

"Great, thanks."

"Let me see the place Dr. Jones needs to remove."

Tom showed her the area on the back of his neck.

"Good. The surgery will not last long, 30 minutes at the most, but you will need sedation."

"OK," said Tom. Linda had read through the information from Dr. Jones's office and had explained to him what to expect.

"You can use the changing booth here. I would like you to get undressed and put this gown on. OK?"

"Do I need to take everything off?" Tom asked.

"It's OK to leave your underpants on, but take your undershirt off."

"You don't happen to know Linda Chance, do you? She's a volunteer in the hospice unit." Tom was trying to find a connection. Dr. Kong had explained to him that the healing relationship extended beyond the physician, and that nurses are often a patient's greatest ally and advocate. Tom recalled their discussion: 'Compete for alliances or risk isolation with little help.'"

"I don't think so. Why do you ask?" Eileen replied.

"She's my wife. She told me that one of the nurses in outpatient surgery plays tennis over at Fairbanks Racquet Club."

"That's Cheryl. She plays every Tuesday. I'm more of a swimmer," said Eileen.

"You look great. Do you swim at the Y?"

"Uh-huh, usually three times a week."

"I never have seen you there. I try to go on Tuesday and Thursday mornings, although I haven't been for the last couple of weeks because of this biopsy. Dr. Smith said it was OK to take showers, but not to get it wet for too long."

"I swim in the master's class three mornings a week," said Eileen.

"No wonder you're in such good shape. Do you mind calling me Tom? It would make me feel a little bit more comfortable. My wife says you guys run the best outpatient surgery department in the city."

"Sure, Tom, and thanks for the compliment. I'll step out while you get changed."

Tom got undressed and put on the hospital gown. *Why do they always keep hospitals so cold?* he wondered. After a few moments Eileen returned and took him in the wheelchair to the operating room.

"Now, Tom, I'm going to start an I.V. on you. I use a needle so it'll hurt a little bit, and then we leave a little plastic tube in your vein so that we can give you medications."

"OK."

"Good morning, Mr. Chance." Dr. Jones entered the room. Did you have an opportunity to read over the information from my office?" Tom noticed the same medical student follow him through the door.

"Yes."

"Do you have any questions?" asked Dr. Jones.

"No," said Tom. *He certainly doesn't seem to be as rushed today as he was in the office.*

"Good. Well, Eileen is going to take good care of you. The first thing we're going to do is give you a sedative through the I.V. This will make you sleepy. Patients often don't remember anything after we give this to them. I do have a medical student with me today who will be observing the procedure. Is that OK?"

Tom glanced over at Grace Freeman and nodded his head as if to say hello.

"Good morning, Mr. Chance." Grace replied more confidently than Tom expected.

Tom looked back at Dr. Jones. "No problem."

"Oh and we won't know the results of the surgery until I see you back in the office in 10 days to remove the sutures. If you have any problems, please call my office."

"Will do. Thanks, doc."

Tom didn't recall the surgery and awoke in the outpatient recovery room feeling cold.

"Hi, Tom. You did great. No problems with your surgery," said

Eileen. "I'm going to bring back your wife to stay with you until it's safe for you to go home, OK?"

"Sure."

"Hey, Tom. How are you feeling?" asked Linda.

"I'm a little sleepy, but other than that I'm OK. I feel a little cold."

"I'll see if Eileen can find a blanket for you. She's been treating you like a king. I understand they don't usually put simple plastic surgery cases in the recovery area closest to the nurse's station."

"She's really nice. She swims over at the Y."

Linda went to find Eileen who was busy attending another patient. Tom closed his eyes. He had never really thought much about relationships until he met Dr. Kong. "Compete for alliances or risk isolation with little help." Tom thought to himself as he drifted back to sleep.

Tom remembered little of the conversations in the recovery room and he recalled the ride home more as a dream, but he felt secure in the care of his wife. *Our relationships help us weather the storms and stresses of life,* Tom thought. They allow us to bend and not break, to stumble and not fall. Our circumstances and situations may change us, perhaps forever, but our connections with others help us survive. He recalled again Dr. Kong's words, "At the heart of healing stands a relationship. The way of nature may force a person from his path, but the strength of that person's relationships draws him back to his purpose and destiny." Tom was beginning to sense the importance of relationships through the insight Dr. Kong had given him of the patient-physician relationship. Slowly, his view of life was changing, and he was beginning to see the invisible world of relationships and how they mold and support every human being.

LESSON ELEVEN

Understand the role of time in the battle against disease. Disease can be deceptive and the opportunity to intervene fleeting. The judgment required to know if your symptoms are serious or not can be difficult to determine. If you are not sure, see your doctor sooner, not later. (See also **www.drpen.com/screeningtests**)

CHAPTER 12

Adaptation

"It does not matter how slowly you go so long as you do not stop."

—Confucius (551 BC - 479 BC)

Tom was looking forward to having the final stitches removed in three days, but he felt apprehensive about getting the report from Dr. Jones. He was coming home from a 'sane' day at the office – no meetings, no conflicts, no crises. In fact, since the Davis deal had gone through without a hitch, he was regarded as the fair-haired boy of sales at GSS. He felt in control of his life – at last.

"Linda, I'm home," Tom called out.

"Hi, Tom. I'm upstairs." Linda was working on a quilt, pinning squares of fabric on a cloth background in a frame to see how the colors matched and preview the pattern. This was a new hobby for her, and she had thrown herself into it with typical Linda zeal.

"Is Michael around?"

"He finished his homework early, so I let him go over to Huan's house. I was going to go get him right now, but if you like, you could pick him up. We're going to have dinner in about an hour."

"Sure. I'll go."

"You know, Tom," Linda said coming down the stairs, carrying handfuls of fabric, "I don't know how to say this, but you've been acting kind of different since you've had all this stuff going on with these doctors."

"Maybe Jones cut out all the bad *yang* in my personality along with the tumor," he teased.

"Well, I'm not complaining. You're just more cooperative, or helpful, or something. I like it!" She paused at the bottom of the stairs and gave Tom an unexpected, lingering kiss.

"I've got to get home early more often," Tom responded appreciatively. "Are you sure Michael isn't home?"

"Don't get too frisky, Lover Boy. We can discuss your 'personality' later tonight."

"Seriously, Linda, I guess I never appreciated all the things that people do for me all the time. I was too busy. Dr. Kong explained it to me this way." Tom took a piece of paper out of his wallet.

忙

Linda sat down and looked at the drawing, clueless. "What's it mean?" she asked.

Tom looked over her shoulder. "The Chinese language uses five different types of characters. This character, "mang," which means "busy," is a pictograph made up of two characters: "xin" which means heart on the left and "wang" which can mean either to flee or run away, or to die. Anyway, when a person becomes too busy, he has run away from his heart. If it goes on for too long, a person can lose his feelings altogether. His heart dies."

"That's sad," said Linda. "We get so caught up in trying to get ahead, we forget to live in the days we're given; then we feel guilty, so we just get busier and run away from how we really feel."

"He's a wise man, but sometimes I lose him because he's always talking in proverbs. I get the feeling that if he had not lived in America for so many years, I wouldn't be able to understand him at all. It's kind of like he's translating his thoughts, but English doesn't have all the right words for them. Anyway, I've been trying to be more focused at work and use my time more effectively, not just for the sake of being busy." Tom gave her a quick kiss on her neck. "I'll go get Michael. See you in a little bit."

The Kongs lived in a modest home less than 10 minutes from the Chances. Tom had never been inside, but today Mrs. Kong greeted him at the front door.

"Good afternoon, Mrs. Kong. "I'm Michael's dad, Tom."

"Come in, Mr. Chance." She bowed slightly. "Dr. Kong and the boys are working in the garden. Could you join us for tea? Dr. Kong and I have tea this time of day. Our son and his wife travel overseas and they are not with us."

"Thank you, Mrs. Kong. I would be honored."

"Please, join the boys outside. I call when ready." Tom found her singsong, slightly stilted English appealing.

"Hi, Michael. Hi, Huan. Good evening, Dr. Kong," said Tom.

Dr. Kong was concentrating on a potted plant and did not respond.

"Dr. Kong is teaching us how to take care of penjing," said Michael. "He teaches Huan every Tuesday afternoon. Some of them are very old, and some of them have been planted in just the last few years. Penjing is the ancient Chinese art of caring for a potted tree. In Japan they call it bonzai, but it originally came from China."

"I see." Tom gazed around at the six or seven potted trees. A bright red oriental maple tree in a green glaze rectangular pot first caught his eye.

"Do you leave them outside all the time?" Tom asked.

"Yes," said Huan. "Penjing live in harmony with nature and demonstrate the power of adaptation. In nature, trees respond to various conditions … wind, water, snow, and ice. The trees adapt by forming various shapes. The art of penjing subjects the trees to forces that mimic nature."

Tom let Huan instruct without interruption. He couldn't help thinking that this boy was a true Kong. *The fruit doesn't fall far from the tree.*

"For example, this spruce twists and turns in the upright, informal style. It struggles to grow toward the sun, but the wind drives it back. Over here, this black pine cascades over the pot as if cling

ing to a cliff's face beaten down by snow and ice and rock falls. My grandfather says, 'A tall tree attracts the wind. The humble survive; the proud perish.'"

"An-Huan."

"Yes, grandfather."

"Now, put this tree in shaded light and give it plenty of water. Good evening, Mr. Chance. Uh, Tom."

"Good evening, Dr. Kong. I have never seen pingjing before."

"*Penjing,* Mr. Chance," Dr. Kong corrected him. "I learned this art as a boy in Shandong, China."

"When did you plant this tree?" asked Tom pointing to an unusually shaped pine leaning to one side with all the branches extending out in one direction.

"I did not 'plant' this tree. I am the twelfth generation to care for this penjing."

"That's incredible," said Tom. "You mean this tree is over 200 years old?"

"My ancestor, Kong Wu Ying, collected this tree from Taishan near the Archway to Immortality over 300 years ago. Constant winds there create the classic wind-swept style of penjing. Authorities wisely no longer allow the collection of trees from the sides of Taishan, but many climb the central way to see the sunrise. The pilgrim on a clear day can see the coast of the eastern sea."

"It sounds like a special place," said Tom.

"I hope once again to climb the steps of Taishan before I am called to follow my ancestors. Over 2500 years ago, Confucius, the most famous ancestor of the Kong family, climbed Taishan and reaching the top declared, 'The world is small.' My generation understands these words better than all previous generations of the Kong family as my brothers and sisters fled the borders of China and abandoned our ancestral home in 1948."

"The war?" asked Tom.

Kong Jian-Shou looked over at the potted tree. "A tall tree attracts the wind. In my generation, the leader of China climbed the steps of Taishan and reaching the top declared, 'The East is Red.'"

"Jian-Shou, the tea grows cold." Mrs. Kong quietly spoke behind them from the small fishpond near the center of the garden. Neither Dr. Kong nor Tom had heard her enter.

"Yes. Come, Tom," said Dr. Kong taking Tom's elbow and breaking the sadness with a smile. "'The world is small.' Perhaps one day you also will climb the steps of Taishan."

LESSON TWELVE

If you believe you have a medical problem, but you are not convinced of your diagnosis or not committed to the treatment plan, ask yourself why. Disease often wins the battle, not from having overwhelming odds, but from effective strategies cast to the side by neglect. Follow through until you are convinced of the diagnosis and committed to win. (See also the Agency or Healthcare Research and Quality's How to Find Medical Information at: **http://www.niams.nih.gov/hi/topics/howto/howto.htm**

CHAPTER 13

The Power of the Name

"They certainly give very strange names to diseases."

—Plato (427 BC - 347 BC)

The tea felt as warm as the autumn afternoon. Tom had not planned to stay outdoors for so long, but he felt comfortable and relaxed. Huan and Michael had started a chess game upstairs. Mrs. Kong was preparing dinner in the kitchen. Tom drank in the setting sun and sipped his tea.

"Now, Tom, we discussed how physicians create a MAP to take the patient from his current condition to an improved condition," said Dr. Kong.

"Yes, and I understand better how the patient helps the physician make his assessment, but how does the physician come up with his diagnosis?"

"A person engages allies when they possess skills and advantages the person lacks but needs for success. Once a patient has decided the disease cannot be managed by nonprescription medications, the patient should contact his physician and not delay. Remember the window of opportunity. If he or she has sufficient concern to contact his physician, the patient should not self-diagnose."

"Not even if the patient is himself a physician?" asked Tom.

"We have a saying in medical school. 'The physician who diagnoses himself has a fool for a doctor.'"

"It's the same with people who act as their own lawyers," said Tom.

"Yes, no doubt. Physicians generate possible causes of disease in their minds and estimate their probability. Uncertainty plagues the process; fear and hope confuse it and make judgment difficult. Physicians suspend their emotions to clarify their judgment.

"Sun-tzu once wrote, 'Warfare follows the way of deception.' So also, the war against illness deceives. The skillful physician pierces the veil of mystery, categorizes the disease, and names it. The name gives the physician power to determine strategy and develop tactics. When the physician gives the patient the name, he empowers the patient to make wiser, better informed decisions."

"How does knowing the name help the patient?" Tom asked.

"Once the physician has given the patient the name, the patient needs to understand the meaning of the name and the character of the enemy he faces. The patient can use three general resources: organizations that advocate for the condition, the local library, or the Internet. The patient should look up the diagnosis and any words he does not understand using a medical dictionary and a medical textbook such as *The Merck Manual of Diagnosis and Therapy.* Merck now provides *The Merck Manual* in both a professional and home edition written in everyday language. Often these two steps alone are sufficient, but if necessary the disease can be researched further online through the National Library of Medicine. More complex decisions regarding treatment can be compared and evaluated according to guidelines available over the Internet from the National Guideline Clearing House. In the past, this process could take hours, but today the information can be gathered over the Internet in minutes. No one can effectively fight a nameless enemy, but patients should proceed with caution and under the guidance of the patient-physician alliance. Going beyond imperils as surely as falling short. Fear paralyzes; innocence betrays."

"You know, Dr. Smith actually did write down something on a piece of paper when he referred me to Dr. Jones. I think I still have it." Tom took out his wallet. "Yes, here it is," said Tom showing it to Dr. Kong.

Malignant Melanoma
Clark's Level II
Breslow Thickness 0.55 mm
Stage I

"Yes. I can show you how to do this on the Internet in my office. Do you have time?" asked Dr. Kong.

"Sure."

They retreated to Dr. Kong's home office and clicked on his online provider.

"First, let's look up the word 'melanoma' at the National Library of Medicine, www.medlineplus.gov. They offer several medical dictionaries, but let's choose Merriam-Webster, as I trust their reputation. Now, if we look up the word 'melanoma,' we find the following definition in the online medical dictionary: "1: a benign or malignant skin tumor containing dark pigment; 2: a tumor of high malignancy that starts in melanocytes of normal skin or moles and metastasizes rapidly and widely-called also *malignant melanoma, melanocarcinoma, melanoepithelioma, melanosarcoma.*" Since Dr. Smith wrote down that your biopsy showed a malignant melanoma, then the second definition names the enemy, 'a tumor of high malignancy that starts in melanocytes of normal skin or moles and metastasizes rapidly and widely'. If we look up the word 'metastasize' we find that we need to look up the root word 'metastasis,' the "transfer of a disease-producing agency (as cancer cells or bacteria) from an original site of disease to another part of the body with development of a similar lesion in the new location."

"You may want to look up other words, such as 'tumor,' 'malignancy' and 'melanocyte,' but the name has told us that you have a skin tumor that has spread from the original site. To understand the character of the enemy we turn to *The Merck Manual of*

Diagnosis and Therapy, the most widely used medical textbook in the world. Merck makes this available for free on their website, www.merck.com. Here we find that a Clark's Level II defines the anatomy of the tumor. In your case, the tumor had spread from the epidermis into the dermis. I'll show you a picture of the anatomy of the skin from the National Library of Medicine in a moment. Dr. Smith told you the level of thickness was 0.55mm. According to *The Merck Manual*, the estimated five-year survival rate for a melanoma of this thickness is 98-100%, and it's treated by surgical excision."

"Wow. Do physicians really want me to know all this stuff?" asked Tom.

"Yes. Physicians not only have a duty to inform their patients, but as we discussed earlier, the physician's assessment must convince the patient before the patient will commit to treatment. Appropriate information convinces the patient of the accuracy of the physician's assessment and helps the patient overcome his fear to take action.

"I see. So that's why a patient who knows the name and definition of the disease can better understand the physician's recommendations and be convinced of the necessity for treatment."

"Exactly. The name unlocks the truth that keeps the patient from getting through the window of opportunity and escaping the attack from the disease. We can learn more from the National Cancer Institute."

Mrs. Kong entered quietly, "Mr. Chance, your wife calls."

"Oh, thank you," said Tom glancing down at his watch. "Where is the phone?"

"Here," said Mrs. Kong handing Tom the cordless phone.

"Hi, Linda, sorry the time got away from me. Michael and I will be right home. Do you need me to pick up anything for you on our way? OK. See you in a few minutes."

"Dr. and Mrs. Kong, thank you so much for your hospitality. The tea was wonderful. Michael and I need to get home for dinner."

"Yes, yes. Please do not let us keep you," said Dr. Kong rising from his chair. "Perhaps I will see you again this Friday at the chess club."

"Yes," said Tom, "Michael and I are coming."

"Good. You are now prepared to understand medical strategy from the patient's perspective. Remember every alliance has at least two partners. Each approaches the enemy differently."

"Thank you. I will see you Friday evening."

Dr. Kong and his wife walked with them to the front door. "Good-bye, Tom. May your years grow as high as the mountains, and your heart be as peaceful as still waters."

LESSON THIRTEEN

Do not self-diagnose. Let the physician diagnose, but DO get the diagnosis from the physician. Have the physician write it down on a prescription pad, then look up the meaning and be sure you understand it. (For further information on what to do after you have a diagnosis, go to the Agency for Healthcare Research and Quality's Now You Have a Diagnosis: What's Next? at **http://www.ahrq.gov/consumer/diaginfo.htm**

CHAPTER 14

The Report

Tom felt apprehensive about meeting with Dr. Jones and asked Linda to go with him. He understood from his last talk with Dr. Kong that the melanoma had been caught early thanks to the insistence of Linda that he see Dr. Smith. Still, the fear continually resurfaced in the back of his mind. What if I'm part of the unlucky two percent who don't survive five years? *What if Dr. Jones finds it had spread further than the first report had indicated?*

He turned to Linda sitting next to him in the car on their way to Dr. William's office and proclaimed, "'Kind words warm a person three winters, harsh words chill the heart even in the midst of summer.'"

Linda was getting used to these proverbs coming from out of the blue. "Another Dr. Kongism?"

"Yes. I think it means 'focus on the positive.'"

They entered the busy office and took their seats. Linda skimmed through a two-week-old issue of *Time* Magazine while Tom tried to appear calm, but his stomach kept reminding him how nervous he felt. They did not have to wait long for Dr. Jones.

"Mr. and Mrs. Chance, please come back with me. Dr. Jones will not keep you waiting long. Is everything going well?" asked the nurse.

"We're doing fine, thank you," answered Tom.

Dr. Jones entered the room shortly. "Good afternoon, Mr. and Mrs. Chance. I have good news for you. There is no evidence of this tumor on the surgical pathology report. I think all of it was removed when Dr. Smith took it off in his office."

"That's great, doctor," said Tom, relieved.

"You do need to follow up with either Dr. Smith or a dermatologist every six months for the next five years. You have an excellent prognosis and we do not expect this particular melanoma to recur, but you need to keep a closer eye on things. You have a higher risk than average for developing another skin cancer."

"Thanks. I'll get it set up. In fact, I have a complete physical set up with Dr. Smith in the next few months. I'll talk to him about it then."

"Good. I'll send him a copy of the report. I've enjoyed taking care of you." Dr. Jones held out his hand. "Let me know if there's anything I can do to help you. My nurse will come in just a few minutes to take out these sutures."

Dr. Jones left the exam room. Tom looked at Linda with a sigh of relief.

"Kind words warm a person three winters," Linda teased. "I guess this will cut down on our heating bill this year."

"Yeah, but I'd rather find another way to be frugal," Tom jokingly replied.

"Are you and Michael going to the chess club tonight?" Linda asked. "Absolutely. It's good for Michael and me. You know, this whole thing has been kind of scary, but I feel like it's also made me grow personally in ways I probably wouldn't have chosen for myself. It's like Dr. Kong once told me, 'Adversity teaches life's most valuable lessons. A kite rises because of an opposing wind.' I really enjoy learning from him."

"He's a wise man."

Tom took Linda's hand and said quietly, "But I really have you to thank, don't I."

This was the man Linda loved. The thought of Susan and Bill brought a rush of emotion. She looked at Tom with moist eyes. "I guess, honey, I just can't afford to lose you."

Dr. William's nurse entered the room and interrupted the moment. "This will just take a few minutes, Mr. Chance. You may feel a little pulling on the skin, but it won't hurt."

"No problem," said Tom.

On the way home they picked up some Chinese take-out for dinner.

"Hi, Mom. Dad. Did everything go OK at the doctor's office?"

asked Michael.

"Yes, dear," said Linda.

"The doctor's visit went *very* well," said Tom. "You know, Michael, your skin is similar to mine. The doctor said I have a higher chance of skin cancer than most people because of the type of skin I have, so you, too, ought to be careful in the sun, especially playing games or out on the water. You should use at least a sunscreen with a Skin Protective Factor of 15 or greater."

"OK, OK, Dad. I just wanted to know how it went, not get a health lecture."

"Alright. Sorry." *How do you teach a fourteen-year-old wisdom?* Tom asked himself. *The young think they are invincible.*

"Let's eat," Linda broke in. "You guys need to leave in half an hour to get over to the library."

LESSON FOURTEEN

The primary tactic used to interpose a defense against disease is vaccination. Know the recommended vaccines for your age group. (For further information, go to **www.drpen.com/vaccines**)

CHAPTER 15

Strategy and Tactics

"In strategy it is important to see distant things as if they were close and to take a distanced view of close things."

—Miyamoto Musashi (1584 - 1645)

"May I have your attention please," said Frank Aldrich. "We are honored tonight to have with us Mr. Dmitry Gurevich from the U.S. Chess Federation. As you may recall, two of our members, An-Huan Kong and Jeremy Adams, did extremely well at the recent tournament in Bethesda, Maryland. Mr. Gurevich visits chess clubs around the country that produce outstanding players, and tonight I have asked him to give a brief presentation on opening gambits.

After the presentation he will be available for game analysis and consultation."

Mr. Gurevich rose from his chair and acknowledged the scattered applause.

"Thank you, Mr. Aldrich. I am very pleased to be here and delightfully surprised to see an old acquaintance, Dr. Jian-Shou Kong. Dr. Kong and I faced each other many, many years ago when he still played chess competitively in New York. I was not aware until recently that his grandson, An-Huan Kong, now follows in his footsteps.

"*Sacrifice a little, gain much* underlies the strategic premise of the gambits, whether one plays the Queen's Gambit, the Danish Gambit, or others. The player sacrifices one, two, sometimes even three pawns to gain tempo in development and positional advantage. For success, however, the opponent must accept the gambit. The rival errs by obtaining an early small material advantage, but then fails to adequately develop his pieces. This creates an excellent opportunity for the player of the gambit to quickly mount an overwhelming assault ending in checkmate.

"Tonight, we'll look at one of the classic examples of the Queen's Gambit, Polson v. Garesov in 1786 . . ."

After Mr. Gurevich had finished his presentation, Dr. Kong motioned for Tom to meet him at the door.

"How did you know Mr. Gurevich?" asked Tom.

"He studied at Columbia when I taught there in the 1960s."

"What did you teach?"

"Medicine. Mr. Gurevich studied anatomy under me."

"Is he a doctor?"

"No, he obtained a master of science in anatomy, but later switched to health administration. After receiving his master of health administration, he developed the organ transplant program at Columbia University. He is an excellent strategist, in business and in chess. We plan to have breakfast tomorrow morning before he flies back to New York."

"I see," said Tom, surprised at Dr. Kong's many sides.

They went over to the coffee and tea shop and ordered two cups of green tea. Tom had cut down on his coffee to two cups in the morning. Now, with the positive prognosis from Dr. Jones, Tom looked forward to learning more about the doctor-patient alliance.

"Every river has two banks, and every alliance has at least two partners. Each approaches the enemy differently," began Dr. Kong. "The physician approaches the disease full of tactical considerations. What is the first choice of medication for this disease? What is the second choice if the first choice fails or has too many side effects? Should surgery be considered? Would allied health professionals, such as physical therapists or occupational therapists, help? The physician approaches disease in this way because tactical feasibility determines strategy.

"And the patient?" asked Tom.

"The patient approaches the disease emotionally and continually fights fear. Knowledge of the enemy justifies fear; knowledge of strategy masters fear."

"I'm sorry, I'm not following you too well, again. What do you mean by strategy? I thought the choice of medication or the surgery *is* the strategy."

"Patience clears a muddied stream."

"I just don't understand the difference between tactics and strategy," Tom insisted.

"The specific actions are tactics; the unifying plan of action to achieve a specific goal is strategy. Does the stream clear?" asked Dr. Kong.

"Yes, I think so," said Tom. "It must be similar to my work in sales. We have specific goals or sales targets that we're trying to reach, and we have an overall plan on how to achieve those goals; but most of our time is spent on short-term actions, what you would call 'tactics.'"

"Yes, but in medicine as in war, winning and losing can have life and death consequences."

"Of course," Tom agreed.

Dr. Kong took a pen from his pocket and wrote on his napkin:

Physicians create a MAP and AIM for specific GOALS.

"You recall how physicians create a MAP with each patient encounter?" asked Dr. Kong.

"Yes," said Tom.

"The MAP explains how physicians draw the bow; the AIM explains how they shoot the arrow." Again, writing on a napkin, Dr. Kong wrote:

Physicians:
Attack to cure or to contain the disease, or
Interpose a defense to block the disease, or
Make an escape to avoid the disease.

Laying the pen down, Dr. Kong continued, "Let me give you specific tactical examples. For infections, if appropriate antibiotics are available, the physician *attacks* to cure the disease. If the infection has produced an abscess or collection of infection, antibiotics have insufficient force to cure, and the physician uses surgery to remove the infection. For viral infections, neither antibiotics nor surgery affect a cure, and the physician uses immunizations to *interpose* an immunological defense against the infection. Patients *make an escape* from sexually transmitted infections by appropriate behavior.

"For cancer, early detection allows the patient to *make an escape* and avoid the consequences of the tumor. While the window of opportunity remains open, physicians surgically remove the tumor to attack and to cure the disease. If the window of opportunity has closed, physicians may surgically remove some of the tumor to block the local effects of the tumor along with chemotherapy and radiation therapy to contain the disease.

"For vascular disease, patients *make an escape* by keeping their cholesterol low either by diet or with medications, by exercising regularly, and by following life-style advice from their physicians. Coronary artery bypass surgery attacks the disease to remove the blockage. Medications work to *interpose* a defense against the effects of the disease."

"I see," said Tom. "Do physicians actually think this way?"

"Yes ... and no," said Dr. Kong. "In medicine, tactics determine strategy because not all diseases have effective treatments. For example, HIV cannot be attacked to bring about a cure because there are no curative treatments available. In this case, physicians strive to contain the disease. Patients should strive to avoid the disease. Understanding strategy helps the patient work together with the physician in an effective healing alliance. Understanding strategy empowers the patient to take action and to master fear. The patient does not always need to understand the details of the particular tactic the physician uses, but the patient should understand the underlying strategy. Proper understanding enables the patient to make a stronger commitment to the treatment plan.

"Physicians approach the disease strategically and tactically while patients must approach the disease emotionally. The patient with strong positive emotions working together with the physician forms a powerful alliance. Working alone with an uncooperative patient renders the physician's best strategy useless. Patients who go against appropriate physician advice abandon their greatest ally."

"I'll accept that," said Tom. "But you mentioned that physicians have specific goals. What are they?"

"Physicians work to improve the quantity or quality of life. All medical strategic plans target one or both of these two goals. For example, a physician creates a MAP on the patient and discovers the patient has high blood pressure. He AIMs to lower the blood pressure by an exercise program or by a medication. In this case, the physician uses which strategy?"

"Well ... isn't he using a defense to block the effects of the high blood pressure?" Tom answered.

"Correct. What is the goal of the alliance?"

"I guess the physician and the patient are trying to extend the quantity of life," ventured Tom.

"Correct again. The physician also has a secondary goal – to avoid any decrease in the quality of the patient's life from side-effects to the medication."

"I see," said Tom. "Physicians assess the problem using the MAP, develop strategy based on available tactics, then AIM for the specific goal."

"Go to the head of the class, Mr. Chance," replied Dr. Kong with a warm smile. "But remember, in any alliance, both allies contribute to overcome the enemy. The best plans of the physician lie powerless without the patient's willingness to follow the strategic plan. A sharp arrow still requires a strong bow. The patient with well-controlled, focused emotions provides the power behind the plan."

Tom sat quietly while Dr. Kong let his understanding take root. After a few moments Tom looked down at his watch and realized it was getting late.

"Thank you, Dr. Kong. I guess not many people understand this, do they?"

"No, Mr. Chance, but we live in a remarkable time. Information now speeds across the world and between nations in seconds. Ancient cultures and modern ideas compete in ways few could have imagined only 100 years ago. But an old tree has many roots. The wisdom of the East will blend with the knowledge of the West. I left China enchanted by the power of western science, but I returned to my roots to rediscover the secrets of how relationships contribute to longevity and happiness. A long life with happiness is a blessing; long life with misery is a curse."

"Dad!" said Michael. "We've been looking all over for you."

"Sorry, son. Dr. Kong and I were discussing some medical concepts, and the time got away from us. Hi, Huan, did you learn anything from Mr. Gurevich?"

"Yeah, he's a great strategist and an expert in positional development. Grandfather, did you really play against him in New York?" asked Huan.

"Yes and no. Actually I was his coach, but perhaps the student has become greater than his teacher."

"Dr. Kong, we've got to get home now. I hope we will see you in a couple of weeks," said Tom.

"Yes," said Dr. Kong. "You do well, Mr. Chance. The height of the wall depends on the depth of the foundation. I think you have laid a good foundation. I hope you enjoy a long and happy life."

Tom and Michael turned to go. For a moment Tom had a hard time understanding his feelings. Then he remembered how he felt when he graduated from elementary school. On the last day his favorite teacher had taken him aside and praised and encouraged him as a boy, wishing the best for him. Today he felt that same sense of warmth as he and Michael stepped out into the cool autumn air under a Chinese blessing.

LESSON FIFTEEN

Know the three main strategies physicians use to **AIM** their tactics in the fight against disease:

Physicians:

A*ttack to cure or to contain the disease, or*

I*nterpose a defense to block the disease, or*

M*ake an escape to avoid the disease.*

Know the two primary goals of physician's recommendations: To improve the Quality of Life and/or the Quantity of Life.

CHAPTER 16

The Advocate

"Prosperity is no just scale; adversity is the only balance to weigh friends."

—PLUTARCH (46 AD - 120 AD)

Tom scratched the back of his neck. The area where Dr. Jones had removed the melanoma had healed well, but occasionally the scar would itch.

"Mr. Chance," the General Software Solutions receptionist called. "There's a young boy who calls himself An-Huan on the phone asking for you. He says it is very important. Should I put him through?"

"Yes, of course," Tom answered. "Hello, Huan. How can I help you?"

"Mr. Chance, forgive me for interrupting your work, but grandfather has been taken to the hospital. My father is away and he is asking if you would come see him."

"Of course. Where is he?" Tom felt his stomach turn.

"He is at the hospital emergency room."

"What happened?"

"He awoke this morning and felt fine. He came down for breakfast, then all of sudden he felt weak and developed severe stomach and back pain. He asked us to take him straight to the hospital."

"Which hospital, Huan?"

"St. Bernadine's Hospital"

"I'll be over in just a few moments."

"Thank you, Mr. Chance. Goodbye."

Tom hung up the phone and told his secretary that an emergency had come up and he needed to go to the hospital to see a friend. St. Bernadine's hospital was less than five minutes from his office.

Tom arrived around 10:00. The hospital emergency room was not busy. He found Dr. Kong in a room near the nurse's station.

"Hello, Dr. Kong, how are you feeling?" Tom asked.

"Tom, thank you for coming. The pain is better now. They have given me some pain medication. My son is away on business, and An-Huan is too young. I need your help."

Dr. Kong looked up from the stretcher deeply into Tom's eyes. "I need an ally."

"How can I help?"

"The doctor has done a CT scan and found that I have a large abdominal aortic aneurysm, a swelling of the large artery in my stomach, that is leaking blood into my back. The bleeding seems to have stopped for now, but it is not stable. I had him write the name down." Dr. Kong handed him the note from the doctor. "I may need to have surgery as soon as possible. I normally go to Georgetown University Medical Center, but they brought me to the closest hospital. All of my colleagues have retired and I do not know the vascular surgeons here. I would like you to get some information to help me choose the surgeon."

"I'll do what I can, but ..."

Dr. Kong lifted his hand to wave off any objections. "The doctor here in the emergency room has recommended Dr. Steven Ward, but he has not been able to reach Dr. Smith to get his opinion. Could you get some information for me to help make this decision? We do not have much time."

"Of course." Tom excused himself. He and Dr. Kong had talked about the best way to choose physicians, but he had not expected to be asked to apply the principles under this kind of time pressure. Tom recalled Dr. Kong's words, 'The patient establishes the patient-physician relationship to create an effective healing alliance. To achieve this goal you must evaluate the physician's character, competence, and communication skills.'

Dr. Kong had told Tom that often health professionals who do not work directly for the physician can be a source of valuable information. Tom also knew a little about the layout of the hospital since Linda worked there as a volunteer and they sometimes had lunch together there. Tom went to the hospital's main floor and spoke to the woman working behind the reception desk. "Excuse me. Could you tell me which floor the vascular patients go after surgery?" he asked.

"I don't know, but the fourth floor is the medical-surgical floor. I'd go there. They should know."

"Would you mind calling them for me? I have a friend in the emergency room and I don't have much time."

"Sure," the receptionist answered. She dialed the number to the fourth floor surgical unit.

"Hello, this is Sharon at the front desk. Could you tell me which floor the vascular patients go to after surgery?"

"The fifth floor? Thanks."

Turning to Tom, she said, "They apparently go to the fifth floor."

"Thanks for your help."

Tom took the elevator to the fifth floor and went to the nursing station. He waited a few moments until one of the nurses came out of a patient's room.

"Excuse me."

"Yes?"

"I apologize for interrupting you. My wife works here as a volunteer. Her name is Linda Chance. Do you know her?" Tom asked, trying to establish a bridge with her.

"I don't think so," she shook her head slightly.

"Well, anyway, I was wondering if I could ask your opinion about something?"

"OK?" She was a little wary of strangers asking for her opinion, but like all nurses she wanted to help.

"I have a friend in the emergency room who needs to have a

repair of an abdominal aortic aneurysm." Tom stumbled over the words as he read from the paper Dr. Kong had given him, then looked back up. "We're trying to decide which surgeon to use."

The nurse was startled by the statement and not sure what the question was. "Why are you asking me? I'm not a doctor."

"I know. But you work with these surgeons every day, and I would just like your opinion."

The nurse led Tom away from the desk as if that would make whatever she said less official. Her voice took on a confidential tone. "As a hospital employee I can't recommend one surgeon over another. The hospital's physician referral office should have all the information you would need as far as training and credentials. Would you like for me to give you their number?"

"Thanks, but I really don't have much time. Like I said he's in the ER right now. Could you just tell me a little about the surgeons who work here?"

"Um, well . . . Dr. Ward is a very good surgeon, and his patients do very well. His office is right next door to the hospital so most of the physicians here use him. But personally I also like Dr. Morgan. Really, all the vascular surgeons are very good."

"Why do you like Dr. Morgan?" asked Tom sensing that this was probably her unspoken first choice.

"Well, he takes excellent care of his patients and responds quickly when called. He also uses some of the newer surgical techniques because he just got out of residency three years ago ..."

"I see."

"... so his patients sometimes get out of the hospital sooner. All of us have commented on how well he communicates with the staff so we always know exactly what's going on and what he wants us to look out for. But like I said Dr. Ward's patients do very well, too."

"That's great. Thanks. Oh, where did Dr. Morgan do his training?"

"Johns Hopkins up in Baltimore."

Tom wasn't finished with his debriefing. "How is Dr. Ward different?"

"Well, don't get me wrong. Dr. Ward is an excellent surgeon. He's been in practice here for at least 20 years. I guess it's really a question of style. He's kind of from the older school. You know, the surgeon *is* the captain of the ship; but some make you feel like you're just following orders, others make you feel like you're a part of the team."

"Is Dr. Morgan's office close by?

"Actually, yes, it's pretty close, just over on High Street."

"Do you have his number?"

"Sure." She returned to the nurse's station and started flipping through a Rolodex. "We keep all the surgeons' numbers here on the floor in case we need to reach them. Here it is. . . Dr. Paul Morgan." She wrote the number on a Post-It page. "I'm also going to give you Dr. Ward's and Dr. Sumaptri's numbers also."

"Thanks. I really appreciate your time. Have a nice day."

"You too, and good luck."

Tom left the hospital and drove quickly back to his office to do a quick search on the Internet. The Board of Medicine in Virginia profiles all their physicians online and he checked the credentials against the American Medical Association's on-line listing for each doctor, then printed out the profiles for both Dr. Ward and Dr. Morgan. Less than an hour had passed. He took the printouts and hurriedly returned to the emergency room.

"Dr. Kong, I talked with one of the nurses on the vascular surgery floor. She recommended Dr. Paul Morgan. I printed the profiles on both Dr. Ward and Dr. Morgan for you."

"Thank you, Tom."

Dr. Kong had just finished reading over the profiles when Dr. Smith arrived.

"Good morning, Dr. Kong. I talked with the ER doctor. How are you feeling?"

"Better. I understand I may need surgery as soon as possible."

"Yes."

"Both Dr. Ward and Dr. Morgan have been recommended. Whom do you recommend?"

"Both are excellent, but I have recently been using Dr. Morgan more often. My patients have been very pleased with his care."

"Yes. Well let us call him and see if he is available. If not, then we will ask Dr. Ward to do the procedure. I know we do not always have the luxury of our first choice in these urgent situations."

"I'll call him now, Dr. Kong."

Dr. Kong turned to Tom. "Fortune favors the prepared mind. Thank you for your help. I am sorry to disturb you from your work. I am in debt to your kindness."

Tom bowed his head slightly. "And I am in debt to your teaching."

LESSON SIXTEEN

Understand the power of loyalty and relationships. A cord of three strands is not quickly broken.*

*Ecclesiastes 4:12

CHAPTER 17

The Gift

"If a man withdraws his mind from the love of beauty, and applies it as sincerely to the love of the virtuous; if, in serving his parents, he can exert his utmost strength; if, in serving his country, he can devote his life; if in his relationships with his friends, his words are sincere – although men say that he has not learned, I will certainly say that he has."

—Confucius (551 BC - 479 BC), The Confucian Analects

Two weeks passed after the surgery before Tom and Linda could visit the Kong family in the hospital.

"Good morning, Dr. Kong, Mrs. Kong," said Tom.

"Good morning, Mr. Chance," replied Dr. Kong in a barely audible whisper.

"May I present my wife, Linda."

"We are honored by your visit, Mrs. Chance," said Mrs. Kong

"Thank you. I've heard so much about your family from Tom and Michael," Linda replied. She had looked forward to this meeting for months.

Dr. Kong's wife bowed slightly and nodded her head. She looked tired. Tom knew from his research that Dr. Kong's chance of survival from surgery for a ruptured abdominal aortic aneurysm had been at best around 10 percent. His stay in the intensive care unit had been especially difficult. He had developed acute kidney failure, then a post-operative pneumonia. Yet, somehow he had survived and was now out on the fifth floor post-op unit where they were allowed to visit him.

"Easy to dodge a spear thrown in the open; difficult to guard against an arrow shot in hiding," said Dr. Kong. "My son, Kong Ming-Zhou, would like to speak with you. He and An-Huan wait in the small room by the nurse's station. I am too weak to visit long with you." He took Tom's hand, then let go and closed his eyes. Mrs. Kong kept her head bowed and her eyes cast to the floor. Linda took Tom's hand and led him out of the room.

Tom recognized the same nurse who had helped him when Dr. Kong was admitted to the ER. "Excuse me," he said. "I don't know if you remember me, but I asked you about doctors here at the hospital the other day – vascular surgeons."

"Oh, yes, I do remember," she said, recalling the excitement of being asked her opinion. "Is Dr. Kong the friend that you had asked for?"

"Yes."

"He's doing exceptionally well for a man of his age. Most patients at his age don't do well with this type of major surgery. His family is so gracious and helpful. We enjoy taking care of him."

"He mentioned that his son was in a conference room. Could you tell me where it is?"

"Sure. Go down the hallway, and it's just before the nurse's station on the right."

"Thanks." Tom and Linda turned to go, when Tom stopped, and asked, "Do you mind giving me your name?"

"Not at all. It's Eileen."

"Thanks, Eileen. Take good care of him. He is a special person."

Eileen smiled and took a small piece of paper out of her white coat pocket. "I know. This morning his wife wrote this down for him to give to me: 'Good fortune hides within the bad; misfortune lurks within the good. Thank you for being our good fortune this day.'"

Tom smiled, "Thanks. I know he'll be in good hands."

Tom and Linda walked down to the small conference room that the doctors use to talk with families. Inside, An-Huan and his father were sitting quietly. When they saw Tom and Linda they stood up.

Huan whispered to his father, "This is Mr. and Mrs. Chance."

"Mr. Chance, Mrs. Chance," said Ming-Zhou Kong, "my family is very grateful for your assistance while I was away, and we would like to honor you with a small gift of our appreciation."

"That's not necessary, Mr. Kong. I was only giving back what I had already received from your father."

"Yes, but it is our way of showing our gratitude. My father asked that I give this to you." He then turned to the desk and lifted up a potted plant. Tom immediately recognized it as the recently planted penjing that Dr. Kong and An-Huan had been working on in their garden. "The mountain pine tree in our country symbolizes 'long life.' This pine bears the marks of the struggle of life and humbly bows over the edge of the pot as if driven down by rocks, snow, and ice, yet the leaves are evergreen, and the tip points always to the sun."

Tom knew he could not refuse. "I am honored" he replied, "and yet, I am unworthy, and I am untrained in the care of penjing."

"An-Huan will help you and Michael care for the tree until you are able to care for it on your own. As we know so well this day, without care, life perishes."

"Thank you, Mr. Kong. Thank you, An-Huan."

Tom and Linda left the hospital carrying the small tree back to their car.

"How old do you think this tree is, Tom?" asked Linda. "It looks kind of old the way it drapes over the side of the pot."

"It is one of the newer plants that Dr. Kong and his grandson had planted together for An-Huan to learn how to take care of them, but you know the Kong family is almost like an institution in China and some of their penjing have been cared for by the family for generations."

"We'll find a good place to put it when we get home."

"I know they don't like too much sun because they can get dried out real easy."

Tom didn't really feel like going back home just yet. "Would you like to go over to the new bookstore on Main Street? They serve tea and coffee."

"Sure, but I would try to find a shaded parking spot so that we can leave the tree in the car. I don't think it would be good for it to get overheated."

"Right."

Inside the huge bookstore, with its coffee and tea bar, Linda and Tom ordered green tea. They decided to split a large blueberry muffin. Their table was near the health section of the bookstore, and Tom decided to browse through the aisle. A book whose cover faced outward caught his eye. He picked it up and read the title.

"Linda," he called in a loud whisper. "Come here."

Linda joined him from the coffee bar.

"You're not going to believe what I found!"

Tom stood in the aisle holding the red covered book as if he had discovered a hidden treasure of great wealth in a common field. On the face of the book in gold lettering was written:

Medical Strategy: The Patient's Perspective

By Jian-Shou Kong

Linda smiled and asked, "A pearl of great price?"

Tom looked up at her and smiled back. "Yes," he said, "or as they say in China, 'words like a guiding light over a darkened sea.'"

LESSON SEVENTEEN

Life is a struggle, and the winners learn how to adapt like a mountain tree beaten down by wind, rock falls, and ice, but always constantly rising to gain strength from the sun. If illness strikes and wounds, focus on recovery. Lean on your caregivers to give you strength. The humble bend and survive; the proud stand alone and perish.

Dr. Kong recovered completely from his operation. His book, *Medical Strategy: A Patient Perspective,* became one of the best-selling books of all time and was translated into over 50 foreign languages. His work transformed and strengthened the relationships between physicians and patients all over the world.

Tom Chance returned to work as a sales representative, but as he studied the teachings of the great eastern philosophers of the past he became an expert on change and how to master the constantly changing workplace through adaptation. He became well-known as a speaker and author on leadership throughout the United States.

Michael and An-Huan continued their friendship through high school and college and remain fierce chess competitors to this day.

Dr. Jian-Shou Kong is a fictional character, and the Kong family does not call the eldest living male relative 'The Living Ancestor.'

The Kong family, the direct descendants of Confucius, lived in Qufu a day's journey from the base of the sacred mountain, Taishan. The Chinese emperors protected the Kong family dynasty after dynasty because they served as the guardians of China's social order. In 1948, however, the first-born son of the 77th generation of the Kong family escaped to Taiwan to avoid "reeducation" at the hands of the Communist Party in China. The 2500-year tradition of Kong residence in Qufu was broken.

Whether a revived form of Confucianism will take root once again in China is uncertain, but Chinese scholars are beginning to make careful reaffirmations of the significance of Confucius's historical role. For example, the statue of Confucius in front of the Kong family temple was restored in 2002 with a ceremony lead by China's current reigning premier, Jiang Zemin.

For those who would like to learn more about Confucius and the Kong family we list the following internet resources:

United Nations Educational, Scientific, and Cultural Organization
http://www.unesco.org/whc/sites/704.htm
http://www.unesco.org/ext/field/beijing/whc/confuciu.htm

ChinaKnowledge
http://www.chinaknowledge.de/guide.html
http://www.chinaknowledge.de/Literature/Classics/classics.htm#kong-congzi
China World Heritage
http://www.cnwh.org/whyc/seconde.htm
http://www.cnwh.org/dbj/enkm1.htm

The First Household Under Heaven
"This popular Chinese book tells the tale of the Kong family. Widely known as the first household under heaven, the Kong family's holdings are enormous. The Kong mansion covers over130 acres and their family temple is known as the grandest family temple in all of China."
http://www.wle.com/products/b847.html

Smithsonian Magazine, The Way of Confucius, November 2001 issue.

ChinaCPC
http://www.chinacpc.com/confucius/hometown-mansion.htm

Signs and Symptoms of Heart Disease

Learn the warning signs of heart disease – it's the number one killer in the West.

"What are the signs of a heart attack? Many people think a heart attack is sudden and intense, like a "movie" heart attack, where a person clutches his or her chest and falls over.

"The truth is that many heart attacks start slowly, as a mild pain or discomfort. If you feel such a symptom, you may not be sure what's wrong. Your symptoms may even come and go. Even those who have had a heart attack may not recognize their symptoms, because the next attack can have entirely different ones.

"Women may not think they're at risk of having a heart attack–but they are. . .

"It's vital that everyone learn the warning signs of a heart attack. These are:

"*Chest discomfort.* Most heart attacks involve discomfort in the center of the chest that lasts for more than a few minutes, or goes away and comes back. The discomfort can feel like uncomfortable pressure, squeezing, fullness, or pain.

"*Discomfort in other areas of the upper body.* Can include pain or discomfort in one or both arms, the back, neck, jaw, or stomach.

"*Shortness of breath.* Often comes along with chest discomfort. But it also can occur before chest discomfort.

"*Other symptoms.* May include breaking out in a cold sweat, nausea, or light-headedness.

"Learn the signs – but also remember: Even if you're not sure it's a heart attack, you should still have it checked out. Fast action can save lives – maybe your own."

– National Heart, Lung, and Blood Institute
http://www.nhlbi.nih.gov

Signs and Symptoms of Melanoma

Often, the first sign of melanoma is a change in the size, shape, color, or feel of an existing mole. Most melanomas have a black or blue-black area. Melanoma also may appear as a new, black, abnormal, or "ugly-looking" mole.

Thinking of "**ABCD**" can help you remember what to watch for:

* ***Asymmetry***–The shape of one half does not match the other.
* ***Border***–The edges are often ragged, notched, blurred, or irregular in outline; the pigment may spread into the surrounding skin.
* ***Color***–The color is uneven. Shades of black, brown, and tan may be present. Areas of white, grey, red, pink, or blue also may be seen.
* ***Diameter***–There is a change in size, usually an increase. Melanomas are usually larger than the eraser of a pencil (5 mm or 1/4 inch).

Melanomas can vary greatly in the ways they look. Many show all of the ABCD features. However, some may show changes or abnormalities in only one or two of the ABCD features.

Early melanomas may be found when a pre-existing mole changes slightly – such as forming a new black area. Other frequent findings are newly formed fine scales or itching in a mole. In more advanced melanoma, the texture of the mole may change. For example, it may become hard or lumpy. Although melanomas may feel different and more advanced tumors may itch, ooze, or bleed, melanomas usually do not cause pain.

Melanoma can be cured if it is diagnosed and treated when the tumor is thin and has not deeply invaded the skin. However, if a melanoma is not removed at its early stages, cancer cells may grow downward from the skin surface, invading healthy tissue. When a melanoma becomes thick and deep, the disease often spreads to other parts of the body and is difficult to control.

A skin examination is often part of a routine checkup by a doctor, nurse specialist, or nurse practitioner. People also can check their own skin for new growths or other changes. (The "How To Do a Skin Self-Exam" section has a simple guide on how to do a skin self-exam.) Changes in the skin or a mole should be reported to the doctor or nurse without delay. The person may be referred to a dermatologist, a doctor who specializes in diseases of the skin.

People who have had melanoma have a high risk of developing a new melanoma. Also, those with relatives who have had this disease have an increased risk. Doctors may advise people at risk to check their skin regularly and to have regular skin exams by a doctor or nurse specialist.

Some people have certain abnormal-looking moles, called dysplastic nevi or atypical moles, that may be more likely than normal moles to develop into melanoma. Most people with dysplastic nevi have just a few of these abnormal moles; others have many. They and their doctor should examine these moles regularly to watch for changes. (Additional information about moles and dysplastic nevi and melanoma risk is available in the NCI booklet What You Need To Know About™ Moles and Dysplastic Nevi.)

Dysplastic nevi often look very much like melanoma. Doctors with special training in skin diseases are in the best position to decide whether an abnormal-looking mole should be closely watched or should be removed and checked for cancer.

In some families, many members have a large number of dysplastic nevi, and some have had melanoma. Members of these families have a very high risk for melanoma. Doctors often recommend that they have frequent checkups (every 3 to 6 months) so that any problems can be detected early. The doctor may take pictures of a person's skin to help in detecting any changes that occur.

– National Cancer Institute
http://ww.cancer.gov

I would like to thank the many people who helped bring The Living Ancestor™ to the reader. First, I would like to thank my wife, Xin-yi Wang Fergusson, not only for her support and love, but for her help in interpreting and translating the ancient Chinese sayings and proverbs used throughout the text. I would like to thank my father-in-law, Wen-lin Wang, and my mother-in-law, Liu-hui for helping me to understand Chinese culture and family and the value the Chinese place on education and practical wisdom. I will always treasure the first proverb my father-in-law taught me on how to find success in life. I would like to thank my Chinese teacher, Wu-ning, for her patience in teaching me Chinese, and the Central Virginia Chinese School for accepting me and allowing me to participate in their children's classes.

I would like to thank Paul Morand for his excellent editorial services in helping me bring out the characters better and for making the story more fresh and alive. I would like to thank Charlie Finley for his dedication and service in revising the first draft. Douglas Payne at Riddick Corporate Marketing has been instrumental in all phases of the publishing process, most notably in the illustrations, cover design, and text layout. How does all that creativity flow out of one person? Joy Blauvelt has managed the project with her usually expert hands, always keeping the project moving forward in a timely manner. I would like to thank Sherry Robertson for her assistance in layout and design, and Dana Jackson for her excellent typesetting.

I would like to thank Bobby Riddick for his insights and oversight. How do so many good ideas come out of one person? I would like to thank Norman Schellenger who has been such a mentor to me as my career has evolved from direct patient care to patient education which has allowed me to reach out to so many more people than I could ever have done in private practice. I would like to thank my former patients. All physicians are ultimately the product of their patients, and my patients have been especially tolerant and understanding of my need to change the direction of my career even though it was often inconvenient for them to find a new doctor. I practiced in my own home town and many of my patients had known me since I was born. I would especially like to thank Meredith House for his friendship, kindness, and honesty in reviewing the text, and for his encouragement to always think beyond the boundaries. Everyone needs somebody who believes in them.

I would like to thank my mother who as a nurse for over thirty years introduced me to the healthcare field, and showed me the important role that nurses serve in healing and in patient care. Nurses serve our communities in so many unseen ways when they are supposed to be "off the job". Love a nurse today! I would like to thank my father who let me grow up and make my own mistakes even when I was not always making the best choices. He was always there to pick me up again when I needed him. You never understand the challenges and trials of being a father... until you become one.

Finally, I would like to thank Donald Sanders, M.D., my partner for over ten years who took me under his wing when I was fresh out of training and showed me how a good and honest physician practices compassionate medicine in an increasingly complex healthcare environment. Many thanks to Jo Bohannon-Grant, M.D., my colleague and friend. Last, but not least, I would like to thank the small group of friends with whom my wife and I meet on a regular basis: Mark and Janet Chase, Michael and Elizabeth Lipford, Bryan and Renee Smith, and Kim and Rhoda Boys. Everyone needs a supportive group of friends who stand by you in times of adversity as well as in times of victory. Truly, for good health and well-being our social relationships are just as important as our professional relationships.

About the Author

Kevin W. Fergusson, MD, MSHA

Dr. Kevin W. Fergusson graduated cum laude from the University of Virginia with a degree in Mathematics before attending the Virginia Commonwealth University School of Medicine on the Medical College of Virginia campus. He is an active member of the American College of Physician Executives, the American Medical Association, the American Academy of Family Practice, the Virginia Medical Society, and the Richmond Academy of Medicine.

After becoming board certified in Family Medicine, Dr. Fergusson went into private practice in his hometown of Richmond, Virginia. As an ardent patient advocate, he became concerned over the changing healthcare system in the United States and the effect these changes were having on the patient-physician relationship. While still practicing medicine full-time, he returned to school and in 1995 graduated with a Master of Science in Health Administration. He was inducted into Phi Kappa Phi National Honor Society in 1995.

In 2000, he founded DrPEN, Inc. (The Doctors' Patient Education Network) which publishes *The DrPEN® Directory*, a guide to finding high quality, professional patient education information on the Internet. *The Directory* helps physicians improve their patients' overall understanding of their health problems and helps strengthen the patient-physician relationship.

Dr. Fergusson is an adjunct professor in the Department of Health Administration at Virginia Commonwealth University on the Medical College of Virginia Campus. *The Living Ancestor*™, a short novel that teaches patients how the relationships with their health professionals influence health and longevity, is his first book.